More Than Strangers

The full-bodied laugh that swept through the room only served to frustrate her more. His penetrating look, raking her with appreciative amusement, missed not one detail, leaving her conscious for the first time of her state of undress.

"Why are you doing this to me?" she asked. "It's absolutely, totally, completely—"

He pulled her into his embrace, laughing eyes glittering. "Jamie," he growled, "you talk too much."

His lips burned over her silken skin. Impatiently, lost and incomplete, her mouth sought his, but he drew back with a husky chuckle. Tugging at a long, dark lock, he tilted back her head.

"Now do you understand?"

More Than Friends

BJ James

FANFARE™

Bantam Books
New York · Toronto · London · Sydney · Auckland

This edition contains the complete text
of the original edition.
NOT ONE WORD HAS BEEN OMITTED.

MORE THAN FRIENDS
A Bantam Fanfare Book

PUBLISHING HISTORY
Bantam Loveswept edition published December 1984
Bantam paperback edition / November 1992

ISBN 0-553-29894-1

Published simultaneously in the United States and Canada

Bantam Books are published by Bantam Books, a division of Bantam Doubleday Dell Publishing Group, Inc. Its trademark, consist-
ing of the words "Bantam Books" and the portrayal of a rooster, is
Registered in U.S. Patent and Trademark Office and in other coun-
tries. Marca Registrada. Bantam Books, 666 Fifth Avenue, New
York, New York 10103.

PRINTED IN THE UNITED STATES OF AMERICA

RAD   0 9 8 7 6 5 4 3 2 1

To the two who have given me much,
but taught me more,
Mother and Dad

Chapter One

Long gray caverns lay in shadow, bounded by towering steel and shielded from the sun. Windows of taller buildings gleamed gold, capturing in reflection the promise of day. Later the brilliance of summer light would beat down on a bustling street, but for now it lay in shade and only three ventured there, barely rippling the early-morning quiet.

"Hiya, Jamie."

"Hi, Bill."

"Early as usual, I see."

"You bet."

Big Bill McClain tossed the last of the cans onto the flatbed of the garbage truck, then turned to watch the small, dark-haired woman as she moved away. He liked the way she walked: saucy and with a dancing rhythm. When she paused before a store window to admire the bikinis displayed there, he laughed and called his choice.

"The red one, Jamie."

"Who, me?" She spun to face him, a look of mock horror on her face. "Wear that little bitty thing? Never!"

"Too bad." Bill winked and turned back to his truck as he called over his shoulder, "You would look terrific in it."

"Ha! That's what you think." Still smiling, Jamie waved again and walked on, reveling in the sounds of the morning. After four long years of the deadly quiet in the isolated French countryside, this was sheer heaven. The smile still curved her lips as she saw the male figure not far ahead. Accustomed to having the street to herself at this early hour, she watched him curiously.

He was moving slowly, his full attention directed to the thick sheaf of papers in his hand. In deep concentration, he hardly looked up as he reached the curb, barely glancing to check for traffic before stepping into the street.

Strangely bemused, almost mesmerized by his athletic grace, Jamie was jerked to a sudden halt by a thunderous crash splintering through the roar of a heavy motor. Spinning instinctively toward the sound, she watched in horror as a massive can toppled from the slowly moving truck. With deadly accuracy, gathering speed as it rolled, it bore down on the lone man crossing the street.

Before it could be lost in the ominous clatter, her shout of warning died on her lips. She realized without thinking that he was too immersed in his reading to heed her cry. Flinging aside her briefcase, she dashed madly toward him. With trained reflexes and the expertise of a girl with six brothers, she launched herself in a flying tackle.

She hit him hard and low, and despite their disparity in size the momentum of her small body took them well away from the path of the can. With a sickening thud they sprawled on the rough asphalt in a tangle of arms and legs. The sheaf of papers he carried scattered in confusion about them.

"What the hell!" The deep husky voice rumbled in Jamie's ear as her head pressed tightly against his ribs.

Startled by the guttural sound, she drew back quickly, trying awkwardly to rise. Equally as startling was the large, strong hand clamping firmly around her ankle, the long fingers encircling it completely, holding her captive.

"Now, little lady, suppose you explain yourself." The rumble had become a low growl, exasperated and intimidating.

Jamie ceased her struggles as her gaze collided with the blazing green eyes that were glaring down at her. Disconcerted by the anger there, she strove desperately for some semblance of composure. "If you would please let go of my ankle, I'd like to move out of the street. This isn't exactly the ideal place to hold a friendly conversation."

"Who said anything about friendly? And it was your idea, honey, not mine. Do you always go around tackling strange men?" His eyes narrowed as, for the first time, he noted her small size. "For a little girl, you

sure pack a mean wallop. Where did you play football?"

"Cute!" Jamie snapped in growing annoyance.
"Look, I'll answer your questions, but must it be right
here?"

"What's wrong with the middle of the street? It's
the spot you chose."

"That's gratitude!" She drew herself up with as
much grandeur as one so small could manage, pointing
to the can that was resting against a lamppost half a
block away. "I should've let *that* run you down."

"Well, I'll be damned! I didn't see or hear it." His
searching gaze returned to her to travel slowly over her
body. Suddenly she was acutely aware that her low-
coiled chignon had been knocked askew, allowing
long dark tendrils to escape. She sensed rather than
saw that her svelte summer suit was no longer immac-
ulate, marred by streaks of dirt and dust. The once perfect bow at her neck was dangling its ends onto the
oil-stained street and the pencil-slim skirt was hovering
at her hips, intimately revealing the length of lightly
muscled thighs. She reached nervously to pull at the
hemline when his eyes abruptly stopped their keen assessment.

"Good lord! Your knee!"

At his words Jamie became aware of a dull throb
at her kneecap. She looked down, horrified to see her
stockings in tatters and blood oozing from a friction
burn. "Ah, rats!" she muttered. "My last pair of
pantyhose."

"Here." A snowy handkerchief was thrust into her

hand. She took it gratefully, dabbing gingerly at the angry scrape.

"Hey! Watch it!" She gasped as she was swung high into a pair of strong arms. She was so preoccupied with her knee, she had not noticed the man had risen to his feet. "Put me down, you big lug!"

"Can't. You saved my life. The least I can do is get your wound treated."

"I did not save your life! Who ever heard of being killed by a runaway garbage can? And I'm not wounded! *Put me down!*"

He ignored her, moving easily to the curb, where he lowered her gently to the steps that led to an office building. "Stay put," he commanded. "I'll gather up my papers, then take you to the infirmary in the Bradford Building."

"I don't need the infirmary. All I need is a Band-Aid and—" She was speaking to empty air. He had deposited her on the steps, given his imperious order, and gone to retrieve his papers. Obviously it never occurred to him that she might not wish to obey.

"I'll show you, you overbearing—" As usual the right word escaped her. As the only girl and the youngest of seven children, Jamie had been exposed to a vocabulary that could make a stevedore blush. But never once when she needed it so badly had she been able to remember a fitting word. "Of all the stupid— Who does he think he is? Where did I play . . . ? Well, the next can . . ."

Jamie muttered unceasingly as she limped the better part of a block, determined to escape the arrogant stranger. Intent on her diatribe, she had no warning before heavy hands grasped her shoulders. In one smooth motion that allowed no time for protest, she was spun around and slung less than gently over a brawny shoulder. With a sibilant whoosh, she lost her breath.

"I told you to stay put," a newly familiar voice chided as hard arms closed tightly across the back of her legs, carefully shielding the torn flesh of her knee.

"Ooohh!" She gasped into his back as she began to struggle in earnest, too blazingly angry to be frightened.

"Be still, Midge." She felt the resonance of his words against her thighs pressed to his chest.

"My name's not Midge."

"Maybe not, but you're a midget, aren't you?"

"Certainly not!"

"You could've fooled me."

"I can tell you this much." She searched for a dignity made impossible by her absurd position. "I'd rather be small than a great hulking giant like you."

"I'd rather you were small too." He chuckled, then laughed, apparently impervious to the vicious pinch she delivered to his side.

"Look." Realizing her struggles were useless, she tried another tack. "I'm perfectly all right. If you'll put me down like a good boy, we can go our separate ways."

"Sorry. Gotta see that your knee is cared for."

"Why bother with the knee? It's the ribs that need attention."

"What ribs?" His long strides, hardly hampered by her slight weight, hesitated for a second.

"The ones you broke when you so *gallantly* threw me over your shoulder," she purred in sweet sarcasm.

"Oops, sorry."

Jamie was quite suddenly tossed into the air. The pavement, the buildings, his laughing face, were all a patchwork blur before she was cradled in his arms, her eyes level with the strong jut of his clean-shaven chin.

"Better?" He grinned down at her, delighted at the stubborn tilt of her chin.

"Not really."

"Where does it hurt? I'll rub it for you."

She gasped as the big hand at her side moved to rest dangerously near the soft swell of her breasts. "You leave my ribs alone!"

A high-pitched giggle followed by a low, deep bark of laughter penetrated Jamie's unsettling frustration. Casting a furtive glance over his shoulder, she became aware that they were the subject of curious scrutiny as the street came alive with people on their way to work.

"Will you please put me down?" She muttered the question into his ear. "People are staring."

"Let 'em stare." With this profound statement, he climbed the steps that led to the Bradford Building. It was here that the numerous offices of the Bradford Corporation were housed, including the one where Jamie worked as a translator.

"Do you work in this building?" she asked.

"Not exactly."

"Well, I do. If you'll put me down, I can get on to work."

"Not yet, Midge."

"Don't call me that! My name's Jamie."

"Hello, Jamie." The dancing green eyes grinned down at her appreciatively. "I was beginning to think you were never going to tell me. My friends call me Mike."

"I'm not your friend, so what do I call you?"

"Uh, that's not nice." He stopped before the elevator and punched the button marked INFIRMARY.

"It's too early. No one will be there at this hour." Her voice rang hollowly in the confines of the express elevator.

"Doc comes in early. He'll be there." With a clang of a bell the door slid open.

Before she could think to protest further, Jamie found herself sitting on the white vinyl of an examining table. She could only blink owlishly under the bright lights that relentlessly banished every shadow from the antiseptic purity of the room.

"Hi, Doc."

"Good morning, Brad. What do you have there?"

"An injured midget."

"I see." Doc peered at her over glasses that perched precariously on the tip of his nose. "Mighty pretty midget."

"Yeah, I know. Take good care of her. She saved my life."

"Oh, did she now?"

"You should have seen her!" Mike embarked on a tale that bore little resemblance to the truth. The can and her tackle grew to such heroic proportions that even the usually solemn Doc smiled. Jamie could only stare in silent wonder.

"Hmm." Doc leaned over her knee, nearsightedly examining the abraded skin stuck firmly to the torn nylon. "I'll have to soak this. Be right back. Don't let her run away, Brad."

"You said your name was Mike," she hissed at him as Doc disappeared from the room.

"It is."

"Then why does Doc call you Brad?"

"Because it's my name." A sensible reply that made no sense, Jamie thought.

"Well, which is it then? Mike or Brad?"

"Why, Midge, I didn't know you cared."

"I don't," she retorted angrily, feeling suddenly out of her depth.

"Since you ask so sweetly"—he grinned as he leaned impudently closer—"I'll tell you. My mother calls me John, the people who work for me call me Brad, and my friends call me Mike. Take your choice."

"I'm not your mother, I don't work for you, and I'm not your friend. Hopefully after today I'll never see you again, so I won't call you anything."

"You can't do that to me." If there had been an award for the Best Wounded Expression of the Day, he would have won hands down.

"I can't what?"

"Desert me."

"Look, John, Brad, Mike—whoever you are—I'm not deserting you. I just never want to see you again." Jamie waved a hand beneath his nose in airy dismissal.

"But I'm yours."

"You're what?"

"There's an old Chinese proverb that says the life

you save becomes yours." A wicked gleam in his eyes
gave the lie to his solemn expression.

"I did not—I repeat, *did not*—save your life."

"You did."

"You're not Chinese." She was sinking in the back-
wash of his lunacy.

"In my heart I am."

Jamie fought the smile. She really did, but this ridiculous statement destroyed her resolve. The corners
of her full mouth trembled in her efforts to suppress it.
The concealing hand she lifted was too late.

"Ah-ha! I knew I'd see that if I waited long
enough. You're even more beautiful when you smile.
Now, what time shall I pick you up for dinner?"

Her smile disappeared as quickly as it had come.
"I'm not going to dinner with you."

"Right." He nodded in agreement. "I'll pick you up
at seven. That should give you enough time to change."
He turned away, ignoring her futile sputtering. "Hey,
Doc, I have to go. Take care of the midget for me."

The last had been shouted over his shoulder as he
left the infirmary. Before the elevator doors closed,
shutting him from view, he held up seven fingers and
winked at a speechless Jamie.

For the first time since she had been hired by the Bradford Corporation, Jamie was late for work. When she
arrived, a deep silence was hovering over the entire office. The girls who worked in the adjoining offices
were mystified by her appearance.

She had not taken the time to change the ripped
stockings, and she walked with a distinct limp. Any

questions that might have been asked were stifled by the stern expression on her face. She moved slowly through the reception area, looking neither left nor right, going directly to her private office. Once the door had closed behind her, she heard the inevitable buzz of curious speculation. With a sigh she sat down at her desk on which her abandoned case lay. Wondering idly who had retrieved it, she drew out her translations and spread them before her.

She had been working half an hour when a tap sounded at the door, interrupting her train of thought. Tossing her pen onto the desk, she called, "Come in."

"Hi, sugar. What on earth happened to you today?" Megan Lawson's curly red head peered around the door, a worried frown on her freckled face. She stepped further into the office, her sherry-brown eyes scanning Jamie for injuries. "One of the girls came to me with this god-awful description of your grand entrance. Are you hurt?"

"I'm perfectly all right," Jamie assured her, "except for the strawberry on my knee and hole in my last good pair of pantyhose."

"Strawberry?"

"Friction burn."

"Oh. Uh, how did you get this strawberry . . . friction burn?"

"Not strawberry friction burn, Meg. A strawberry *is* a friction burn."

"Okay." Meg paused for a beat. "So how did you get it?"

"I tackled a madman."

"Okay, I'll buy that. Just where was it you tackled this madman?"

"In the street."

"You mean, the street as in the middle of?" Meg's expressive eye brows rose a notch.

"Smack-dab." Jamie nodded.

"Okay, fine. I'll buy that too. Now, why did you tackle this madman smack-dab in the middle of the street?"

"Because he didn't hear the garbage can."

"Okay, wait a minute." Meg's eyebrows rose again, threatening to disappear into her hairline. "I think I must have missed something here. Maybe you'd better tell me again."

"If you'll stop saying okay every other breath and listen for a minute I'll explain. This nut was crossing the street when a can fell off Bill's truck. I didn't have time to warn him, so I knocked him down," Jamie explained patiently.

"Ah-ha! You knocked him down so the can couldn't!"

"Right."

"When did you discover he was a madman?"

"Right after I knocked him down."

"Not a smart move, huh?"

"Not exactly. Next time I'll let the can have him."

"What did he look like?"

"I don't really remember. He was tall, maybe six four or so. His hair was light brown and waved just a bit, mainly because he needed a haircut. Judging from the crook in his nose, I'd guess it's been broken more than once. His eyes were the greenest I've ever seen, and he had a tiny scar at the corner of his mouth. On the right I think. He had a heavy beard and probably needs to shave twice a day." Jamie paused, unaware of the sparkle in her eyes. "And he wears Grey Flannel cologne."

"Gee, too bad you didn't get a better look at him." Meg giggled, her red curls bobbing gleefully.

"Meg," Jamie said in a warning tone, and glared at her, "don't you have something you need to do?"

"Okay—oops. Sorry." A mock salute accompanied the apology, the giggle now a wide grin. "Message received. See you later."

After Meg had gone, Jamie sat for a long while, staring down at the words before her, not seeing the black and white of ink and paper. In her mind was brown, wavy hair that needed a trim and green eyes with the fire of emeralds. The scar at the corner of his mouth—was it right or left?

"Blast it, Jamie, have you lost your mind?" she said, and snatched her pen from her desk. She began to work furiously, determined to wipe his devilish image from her mind. She worked intensely for the remainder of the day, not stopping even for lunch. By five o'clock she was tired, hungry, and extremely irritable. She looked up with annoyance when a tap sounded at the door.

"Yes?"

"Delivery for Miss Jamie Brent."

"I didn't order anything."

"You *are* Miss Brent?" The young boy at the door held a large package with the wrappings of one of the city's largest department stores.

"Yes, I am."

"Then the package is yours."

"But—"

The boy had gone as quickly as he had come. Jamie stared at his retreating back for a moment. Then, intrigued despite herself, she began to strip the paper from the box.

"Oh, no!" In it were six dozen pairs of stockings in exactly the right size. Written on the small card tucked in the tissue was *John, Brad, and Mike.* The bold black scrawl was as impudent as the man himself.

"He *is* a madman!" Hurriedly, curiously unnerved, she gathered up her purse. Ignoring the box and her papers still scattered over her desk, she left her office.

The corridors were filled with people eager to call an end to the working day. Snatches of conversation were tossed back and forth as the crowd converged on the elevators. Always reluctant to be a part of the melee, Jamie was even more so today. Hoping to avoid the stares of her fellow workers and the probing questions that would inevitably follow, she ducked into the secretaries' lounge. She spent long minutes smoothing back her hair, and after adjusting a pin or two, she sat down to wait a few minutes more.

"Hi, Jamie."

Jamie's dark image was joined in the mirror by the coolly blond reflection of Lisa Lang. Lisa, a notorious flirt, made no secret of the fact that she was in the market for a rich husband—the richer, the better. She and Jamie had never spoken except to exchange greetings in passing. They shared no common interest, for what Lisa wanted most, Jamie wanted least.

"Hello, Lisa."

"He's gorgeous, isn't he?"

"I beg your pardon?"

"I said, he's a gorgeous hunk."

"Who?" Jamie's puzzled eyes met Lisa's in the mirror.

"The man you were with this morning."

"Oh." Jamie shrugged. "He was fairly handsome, I suppose."

"Fairly? You *suppose*? You've gotta be kidding." Lisa's eyes narrowed speculatively. "You don't know, do you?"

"Lisa," Jamie began impatiently, "what is it I don't know that you seem to feel I should?"

"You can't be serious." The china-blue eyes were incredulous.

"Look, you obviously followed me here for a reason. Would you like to get to the point? Then maybe both of us would understand what this conversation is about."

"Never mind." Lisa checked her makeup one more time, brushed back her sleek long hair, and strolled provocatively to the door. With her hand on the knob she turned back to face Jamie. "Since you don't want him, you won't mind if I go after him, will you?"

"Be my guest. You can have him."

The door swung shut, leaving Jamie alone once more. A perplexed frown creased her normally clear forehead. This had been a strange day. It had started with a madman and ended with a gold-digging sexpot. She shrugged wearily, checked her watch, and rose. It was five-thirty. By now most of the rush to leave the building would be over.

The hallway was empty as Jamie walked slowly to the elevator. The usual staccato of her spike heels had a definite hitch. In the quiet the hushed efficiency of the express car was unnaturally loud as the door glided open and Jamie stepped into the lobby. She checked the interoffice mail slot for any late messages, then made her way to the exit.

To her surprise there was a small group of men and women milling about in the street by the revolving door. This in itself was strange for the time of day. She was curious, but not suspicious as she stepped hesitantly through the door, hoping to pass through the crowd unnoticed.

A woman detached herself from the group, making a quick grab for Jamie's arm. "Are you Jamie Brent?"

"Why, yes, I am."

"Here she is, boys!" The bellow was heard by the people Jamie had hoped to avoid. They converged in a swarm, pushing, shoving, each trying to be closest to her. Flashbulbs popped and a microphone was shoved under her nose.

"Is it true that you rescued the city's wealthiest man from certain death this morning?"

"I beg your pardon?" She tried to push the microphone away.

"Come on, girlie, don't be coy."

"Why were you with him so early? Had you made a night of it?"

"There must be some mistake. I—I don't—" Jamie stuttered to a surprised halt.

"Are you his latest lady?"

"Would someone please tell me what—" Another flashbulb exploded in her face, blinding her.

"What's it like to be involved with a man like Bradford?"

"Please, I . . ." Jamie could hardly speak as bewildered tears gathered in her eyes.

A screech at the curb followed by the slamming of a car door drew attention away from her. A tall, imposing man moved arrogantly through the crowd as a reporter tried one more question.

"Are you Bradford's lover?"

"What?" Jamie snapped, no longer bewildered as stunned disbelief flared into white-hot rage.

"Sorry I'm late, Midge." She was scooped off her feet into powerful arms that held her protectively against a granite-hard chest.

"It's Bradford!" The group fell silent as the proud man stared down at them.

"Put me down," Jamie muttered in his ear, her confusion trembling in her voice.

"Henderson!" Mike's roar startled her, and she knew that he had not heard her protest. The green eyes that blazed down at the unfortunate Henderson were filled with barely controlled fury.

"Yes, sir, Mr. Bradford?"

"For that last question I will expect the lady to receive both a verbal and a written apology. Is that understood?"

"Yes, sir."

"Good. Now, as for the rest of you. Miss Brent and I have no definite plans, but when we do a formal statement will be issued. Until such time you will treat her with the respect due my fiancée."

"Your what?" Jamie's gasp was muffled as her head was pressed firmly into the soft fabric of his blazer.

"Hush, Midge." Holding her close, he shouldered his way through the reporters. At the car, illegally parked at a bus stop, he turned back to add one more comment. "Miss Brent has had a trying day. I'll expect you to respect her privacy both now and in the future."

Astonished by all that had happened, Jamie offered no protest. With her composure demolished, she found herself seated in a sleek low-slung car that sped away from the curb.

"Are you all right?" The fury had gone from him; his voice was gentle.

"No. I don't think I'll ever be all right again."

"Did anyone hurt you?"

Jamie could hear the promise of danger for any who might have done her harm.

"Not physically."

"Thank God!"

"For what?" She huddled deeper into the rich leather of the seat. "You've just brought the ruin of my reputation, probably cost me my job, and destroyed my private life. And how dare you tell them that I was your fiancée?"

"Would you rather have them think you were my lover?" The quiet question had the impact of cold steel.

"Certainly not!" Renewed anger stiffened Jamie's spine. Her securely pinned hair threatened to spill free as her head jerked toward him.

"Then what better way to squelch the rumor than to let them think I'm going to make an honest woman of you?" He was so maddeningly calm that she wanted to hit him.

"What ever did I do to deserve this?"

"Cheer up. It could have been worse." Laughter laced his words.

"Tell me how." She moaned as she slumped again, dejectedly, in her seat.

"You could have broken your leg, Midge."

"That would have been distinctly preferable."

"Why?"

"Simple. Then an ambulance could have taken me to the hospital and no one would have seen you hauling me about like a sack of potatoes. There would have been no Lisa and no reporters."

"Jamie, I'm sorry about the reporters."

"You mean, you didn't call them?" The sarcastic edge in her voice brought a frown to his face.

"No." He spoke softly and quietly. "Your privacy is safe with me. *And* your reputation *and* your job."

"My job?" The obvious at last penetrated her unthinking mind. She sat bolt upright, her look incredulous. "Bradford! You're a *Bradford!*"

"I'm afraid so."

"You said you didn't work in the Bradford Building," she accused.

"I don't, but I have connections there."

"Great! Just what I need to make my day complete—a lunatic with connections."

"Sorry, Midge," he said softly as he smothered a smile.

They rode for several blocks in silence. Jamie slumped lower in the seat, mourning for the peaceful life she suspected would never be hers again.

"Who's Lisa?" he asked.

"Who's Lisa?" In an effort she pulled her mind from her chaotic thoughts.

"That was my line, Midge." A velvet chuckle, deep as night, surrounded her.

"Don't call me Midge! And would you please stop talking nonsense."

"You said that if you'd broken your leg, there would have been no Lisa. Who's Lisa?"

"She's a girl I gave you to."

"Ah-ha! So you do admit I'm yours."

"No, I don't."

"Then how could you give me away?"

"I didn't."

"Then you want to keep me for yourself." There was a tenderness in his voice that struck a responsive chord that frightened as well as thrilled her.

"Yes ... I mean, no ... I ... Oh! Just shut up!" Jamie squeezed her eyes shut, willing him away. Then she opened her eyes wide to stare at him.

"Yes, ma'am," he said, and a satisfied smile crept across his rugged features.

Silence descended again and neither spoke. The Corvette was expertly wheeled through all the proper stops and turns. When they drew to a halt at the curb in front of her apartment, Jamie was too distressed to ask him how he had come to know her address.

She had fully intended to be out of the car and into the building before he could stop her, but her injured knee and the fact that for a big man he was exceptionally fleet of foot defeated her. She was, for the third time, lifted into his arms and cradled against him.

"Would you please stop doing this?" she asked between clenched teeth.

"I can't. I'm honor-bound to take care of you."

"You don't owe me a thing."

"Yes, I do. You wouldn't have hurt your knee if it hadn't been for me."

"There are a lot of things that wouldn't have been hurt if it hadn't been for you."

"Like what for instance?"

"Like my pride, my reputation. How are those for instances?"

"See! You do need me. But relax, honey, you're in my hands now. I'll take care of everything." He laughed confidently and Jamie longed to slap the smug look from his face.

"I'll just bet you will," she muttered.

Carrying her easily, Mike crossed the lobby. Jamie cringed at the sight of Mrs. Horton, the resident busybody and chief gossip. She had no doubts that his disgusting escapade would be the talk of the entire population of the building by morning. She closed her eyes, trying to forget the raised eyebrows and pursed lips on the avidly curious, elderly face.

"Good evening, Jamie."

"Good evening, Mrs. Horton." Jamie sighed and blushed under the weight of the old woman's interest.

"Good evening, Mrs. Horton." Mike greeted her cheerfully without breaking stride.

"Good evening, young man."

"Now you've done it!" Jamie grumbled in a low whisper as they moved into the waiting elevator.

"What have I done?" His was a stage whisper, easily heard through out the lobby.

"That, you grinning ape, was the biggest gossip of the building."

"Then by all means, let's give her something to gossip about." The elevator doors were barely closing, leaving them in view of Mrs. Horton as he bent his head to capture Jamie's lips in a kiss. The car was well on its way before he lifted his head, only to lose himself in the shimmering sapphire of her eyes.

"Just for the record, are you hell-bent on the total destruction of my reputation?" Jamie retreated behind a shield of anger, her voice rising to a quavering note as her heart pounded in a strange rhythm.

"No, ma'am." He was falsely contrite. "I just wanted to give the little old lady a thrill."

"You certainly did that!" Jamie suffered the rest of their journey in aggrieved silence, speaking only when necessary and in short, terse sentences. At her door she stirred in his arms.

"You can put me down now."

Slowly, reluctantly, he set her feet on the floor, but his hand stayed at her side. "You rest for an hour, or do whatever it is women do to get ready for dinner, and I'll be back at seven."

"Wait, Mike—uh, Brad—or whatever your name is. I truly don't feel up to going out. My knee hurts and all I want is a nice long soak in the tub."

"Okay."

"Okay? You mean, it's really okay? Oh, hell," she

muttered, "I sound like Meg. That's it, then? You aren't going to argue?"

"Why should I argue?" His wicked grin should have warned her, but Jamie had victory in sight and it blinded her.

"No reason," she answered blithely with a wide smile. "Good night, whoever you are." The door closed between them, and for the first time that day she felt safe from his bewitching charm.

"Thank heaven today is finally over." She removed the pins from her chignon as she walked to her bedroom. The long, heavy coil of her hair spilled down her back like black satin. With weary fingers, she massaged her aching neck. The sheer weight of her hair could feel like a ton. Jamie knew she shouldn't pull it back so harshly, but there was no other way to manage the riotous curls that would spring up if not tightly controlled.

Her hair was again off her neck, this time in a ponytail, when the doorbell rang.

"Oh, rats!" She reached for a towel and rose hurriedly from the tub. "Who on earth could that be?"

In a matter of seconds she was at the door, dressed in only a light robe of cranberry silk. An insistent ring of the bell was accompanied by an imperious knock, and in anger she flung the door wide.

"Oh, no." She stared in dismay into the laughing eyes that had been haunting her all day. "What are you doing back here?"

"You were too tired to go out for dinner, so I brought dinner to you." He turned to a mysterious figure hovering in the background. "J.C., bring on the chow. The lady's hungry."

"What?" Jamie could say no more. She was snatched, quite unceremoniously, out of the way and held tightly while she watched in utter amazement.

Two men entered and worked with practiced finesse. They assembled a brass and glass table, covered it with a delicate lace cloth, then set it with fine crystal, silver, china, and a small bouquet of daisies and ivy as a centerpiece. Two dainty chairs were put in place, followed by a tea cart bearing cartons marked Jean-Charles. The last thing to arrive was a silver bucket filled with ice and two bottles of wine.

"That's good enough. The lady and I will serve ourselves."

"Fine then, Mike. If there's nothing else, I will say good appetite and good night," the man who'd set the table and placed the food said. With a bow to Jamie and a subtle wink for Mike, he commanded his assistant to follow him from the room.

Jamie did not speak until the door had closed and they were alone. "That was Jean-Charles himself?"

"Of course."

"But how did you ...? I mean, why did he ...? I—"

"Jamie. Hush."

He set her gently on her feet. His dancing eyes swept over her, missing not the slightest detail. She blushed under his intense gaze and to her everlasting disgust she fidgeted like a bashful schoolgirl.

"What?" She dodged the hand that lifted to her hair.

"I've been wondering all day what this glorious mass of black hair would look like released from that knot." He pulled loose the ribbon that was holding her ponytail and her hair tumbled over her shoulders. "Mmm, lovely."

"Stop!" She jerked back from the hand that was burying itself in the shining silk.

"Jamie?" He brought his face close to hers, his lips only a heartbeat from her soft mouth.

"Yes?" Her voice had grown husky and her eyes were sparkling sapphires as she looked deeply into the green fire of his.

"Let's eat. I'm hungry."

"You're"—she swallowed convulsively—"you're hungry?"

"Disappointed?" he asked in lazy amusement.

"Why should I be disappointed?"

"Because I didn't kiss you."

"That's ridiculous." Jamie indignantly drew herself erect, anger flushing her cheeks.

"Don't lie, love, or your nose might grow."

"Why of all the conceited . . . conceited—"

"Idiots?"

"Yes, idiots. Thank you."

"You're welcome. Now, come eat while the food's still warm."

"I'm not hungry." She folded her arms stubbornly across her breasts.

"Yes, you are, you skipped lunch today." His hand at her shoulder guided her nearer the table.

"How did you know that?"

"Never mind, it's not important. Now, come eat or

I *will* kiss you. And I won't stop with a kiss, believe me."

"How dare you—"

"Jamie, don't you know that the better part of valor is knowing when to retreat? Now, come eat your dinner."

Chapter Two

In the flickering candlelight Jamie watched him warily. The craggy planes of his face were rough-hewn and implacable. She sensed that he was a man of strength who would choose his path, set his goal, and never deviate. His was a confident power, made greater by tenderness and humor. Before the sumptuously set table, his masculinity was not diminished, but enhanced by the dainty chair on which he sat. Beneath the mischief showing in his expression lurked an underlying sincerity. As she watched him he watched her, his eyes glittering with laughter and something more.

Jamie touched the petal of a daisy nestled among the ivy in the nosegay that graced the center of the table. Its velvet smoothness was a premonition of the touch of his lips against hers. At the thought she trembled, and her gaze was irresistibly drawn to him. His hand covered hers; their eyes met and held.

"Who are you?" Her unbidden thought was spoken.

"Who I am depends on who I am to be to you."

"As in mother, co-worker, friend?" She laughed nervously.

"Yes." His searching look roamed her face, keenly alert to every nuance of her expression.

"One is impossible, the others are unlikely," she drawled.

"My name is John Michael Bradford," he offered softly and waited, perfectly calm in the quiet that followed.

"Mike," she chose at last.

"Friend?"

"Yes."

"It will do." Silence stretched again between them. Then when she thought he would say no more, he spoke softly. "For now, it will do."

Barely taking his eyes from her face, he lifted the wine from the cooler and filled the fragile long-stemmed glass at her place. Jamie had the strangest sensation that something of major importance had been settled, that he had taken her measure and not found her lacking.

"J.C. will never forgive us if we let this food go to waste and I'm starving. Midgets may not each much, but we giants do."

"My goodness! How did you know?" Jamie gasped as he lifted the covers from the silver chafing dishes. "These are all my favorites."

"Just a lucky guess."

"No." She studied him closely. "I don't think so. You don't leave anything to chance, do you?"

"You know me pretty well already, don't you? All right, I confess. I called your friend Megan."

"How did you know about Meg? You and I just met today. How can you know so much about me? You know I skipped lunch, you know Meg is my friend. You even sent the right size in—Oh, no! The pantyhose! How did you know what size to send? Good grief, do I have any secrets left? Is there nothing you don't know about me?"

"The pantyhose were the easiest part. I just told the clerk that I needed some that would fit a very slender midget."

"You didn't!"

" 'Fraid so."

"I must be the laughingstock of the entire city." She groaned. "This has definitely not been one of my better days."

"This has been the best day in both our lives," he contradicted.

"That's a matter of opinion. Maybe it was a good day for you. You didn't rip your pantyhose."

"I hope not."

"Or get a strawberry on your knee."

"A strawberry?"

"A friction burn."

"A strawberry . . . a friction burn?"

"I've already had this conversation one time today." Jamie sighed.

"I'm only teasing, honey. I know what a strawberry is, and I know from experience how painful they can be."

Jamie continued her list of grievances. "And you didn't get backed to the wall by a mob of howling, ugly reporters."

"I'm sorry about the reporters. By tomorrow I should know where they got their information." His voice had grown cold. Jamie could almost feel sorry for the one responsible. Almost.

"What will you tell them?" she asked softly.

"Who?"

"The reporters, of course."

"Why should I tell them anything?"

"Mike." Jamie was exasperated by his feigned obtuseness. "You know you promised them you would release a formal statement when we had definite plans."

"I will."

"When?"

"When we have definite plans." There was an odd look in his eyes, as if he were waiting for something.

"Just a minute! Just a damn minute!" Jamie slammed her hand, palm down, onto the table. "What are you talking about? What definite plans?"

"The plans for our wedding, of course."

"There are no wedding plans," she snapped.

"Not yet, but it's only a matter of time."

"Never!"

"Yes. Soon." It was a promise as well as a contradiction.

"You listen to me, whatever your name is, and you listen closely. First thing tomorrow you call the papers and tell them that we are not, nor ever will be, getting married."

Mike shook his head sadly. His smiling eyes filled with pity, his lips quirked indulgently, tenderly.

"Don't you sit there and shake your head at me!" Jamie was nearly shrieking. "This is all your fault. If you'd left me alone this morning, none of this would have happened."

"Jamie?" The quiet voice intruded on her tirade.

"What now?"

"Had you rather they think you're my mistress?"

"Oh, no," she moaned with her eyes rolled to the ceiling.

"Then I can't tell them we aren't getting married."

"I know I'm going to hate myself for asking, but why?"

"Because we were together so early this morning, they assume we were together through the night. That leads to what they consider an obvious conclusion, that you're my mistress." His suddenly stern expression softened at her stricken look. "I'm sorry, honey. I know it isn't fair. You did a good deed and it blew up in your face."

"I should have let the can have you," she muttered.

"But you didn't, and now you have me."

"Would you please stop saying that? You are *not* mine. I don't want you or any man. I've had enough of men to last me a lifetime. Just go away." She pushed away her plate. "Take your fancy trimmings and just go."

"What men?" He had gone utterly still, nothing

moving but the slow rise and fall of his chest. When she did not respond, he repeated with deadly gentleness, "What men?"

"Ha! Is that a little detail your spy missed? Were you not informed of my wild social life and the seven men in my past?"

"Seven?" He relaxed, but only slightly. "You have six brothers. Who was the seventh man?"

"Stop it!" She rose from the chair abruptly, nearly toppling it over. Resting her hands on the table, she leaned toward him, anger in every look and every gesture. "Who are you to pry into my life? Who gave you the right to question me?"

"You did, when you made my life yours."

"You are the most aggravating, conceited, annoying . . . annoying—"

"Blockhead?"

"Yes, blockhead. Thank you."

"You're welcome. Now, tell me about the seventh man."

The cry of pure frustrated rage that ripped from Jamie's lips startled her. This man, this stranger, had her completely off-balance. The rigid control she had long ago learned to exert over herself and her emotions was rapidly slipping away. She walked to the open door. Stepping out on the small terrace that overlooked a tiny creek, she breathed deeply, willing herself to regain her composure.

In the waning light she was an image of feminine grace. The cranberry silk of her robe clung softly to the gentle curves of her body, its vivid color a becoming contrast with the raven's wing darkness of her tumbled hair. Her profile against the deepening blue of the sky was sweetly regal. The high forehead, marred by a frown, was marked by brows as black as her hair. Blue eyes, flashing sapphire, were fringed by heavy, thick lashes that easily brushed the satin curve of her cheek. A tip-tilted nose made impossible the sophistication she sought, but any who doubted her depth of character had only to note the strong cut of her chin, jutted at a defiant angle. Despite her trembling rage and the hovering tension within her, she was lovely.

The robe, properly demure in cut and style, covered her from neck to toe. Only her body, the way she moved, and the way she stood made it sensually alluring. With her bare toes peeping from beneath the hem and her black hair never more beautiful than in this tousled cascade, she was a woman created for love. And the man who watched her became more determined that she would be his.

"Jamie." He rested his hands gently on her shoulders, ignoring how she tensed at his touch. "I didn't pry into your life. I simply read your résumé. It's almost a matter of public record, and I really know only minor details. That you graduated from college with a degree in physical education, that you're a qualified teacher and you taught four years."

A lazy hand brushed back the locks that curled helter-skelter about her shoulders. "I know that you had all the obligatory childhood diseases." His hand touched lightly at her right arm. "I know you broke this arm when you were sixteen and your left ankle when you were twenty. You're twenty-six years old, five-feet-one."

"And a half."

"Yes, let's not forget that all-important half inch." The smile that lit his face was infinitely tender. "You weigh ninety-five pounds if you think heavy. You came straight from France to the position you have now. And, no matter how hard you try to deny it, you're a warm and loving lady, beautiful inside and out."

"That must be quite a résumé." Her anger was cooling before his quiet calm.

"I could see the last part for myself."

"That's impossible. We've only just met. We haven't even known each other for a day yet," Jamie protested.

"How long does it take, Jamie? Is there a pre-scribed time? A set number of days, hours, or minutes before two people can see that they belong together?"

"You're absolutely mad! Insane!" She turned to face him, her eyes wide with confusion.

"No, love, I'm not insane. It isn't insanity to feel that I belong to you. You're still fighting it, but deep in your heart, you belong to me too."

"But I don't know anything about you," she whispered. In her agitation she failed to notice the flicker of satisfaction that crossed his face when she did not deny the truth of his statement.

"The night air is chilly and you're not properly dressed. Come inside and have your coffee while I tell you about myself. I'll tell you anything you want to hear. There's nothing you can't ask me." The arm he draped around her shoulders to guide her back inside was proprietary in its care.

"Now," he began after he had her seated comfortably, a cup of fragrant coffee in her hand, "you already know that I'm John Michael Bradford. In a few weeks I'll be thirty-three. I stand six two in my bare feet. After four years of playing football for Georgia Tech, I graduated with a degree in electrical engineering."

"Is that how you broke your nose? Football?"

"Twice."

"And the scar on your lip?"

"A woman gave me that."

"A woman!"

"Yes." His eyes crinkled, and a pleased smile deepened on his face. She knew then she had fallen into his trap, her reaction what he had wanted. "An older woman. I was six, she was seven. We had a slight difference of opinion, and due to her superior age, she won."

Jamie laughed. Like the notes of a crystal bell, it filled the room, dispelling the last remaining tension. She relaxed, her eyes meeting his as she sipped her coffee.

"Any more questions?"

"Not at the moment, but I reserve the right to ask more in the future."

"Then we have a future?" he asked softly, his eyes never leaving her.

"I don't know."

"Progress! At last!" The slap of his hand against his knee shocked her.

"What on earth are you talking about?"

"Less than an hour ago you were violently declaring you never wanted to see me again. Now you seem less certain. That means you're closer to admitting the truth."

"Don't start again. We've settled that." The tension was back; her expression had grown determined. "I think I made myself perfectly clear. There's no room in my life for men. Not now, not ever."

"Not men, Jamie. Man! Me!" He took her cold hand in his. Gently he opened her fingers one by one, then laced his own through them. The clasp was tender and possessive. "Don't fight the inevitable, Midge. It's meant to be. I was given to you this morning just as surely as I sit before you now, alive and unharmed."

"Well, don't tie a yellow ribbon around your neck too soon. If you count your chickens before they hatch, you just might find this bird in the hand doesn't want the deed signed, sealed, and delivered."

"Jamie, darlin'." He was smiling, not the least perturbed by her vehemence. "You fractured no less than four proverbs."

"I'm going to fracture more than a proverb if this conversation continues."

The full-bodied laugh that swept through the room only served to frustrate her more. His penetrating look, raking her with appreciative amusement, missed not one detail, leaving her conscious for the first time of her state of undress. At her telltale blush the smile that lifted his lips deepened in maddening perception.

"You are the most infuriating—"

"And you"—a big hand reached to pluck her bodily from her perch at the sofa's edge, holding her easily on his knees—"are the most adorable—" A teasing kiss was brushed over her throat.

"Stop that!"

". . . marvelous." His lips feathered lightly across her brow.

"Let me go."

". . . beautiful." Ignoring her struggles, he traced a path of fire from her brow to a delicate, shellike ear.

"D-don't."

". . . delicious." Strong teeth nipped lovingly at the tiny earlobe, his warm breath sending shivers down her spine.

"Mike?"

". . . exciting." Fleeting and tantalizing, his lips touched hers.

Desperate, Jamie pulled away, her lips burning from his caress. "Why are you doing this to me? It's absolutely, totally, completely—"

He pulled her back into his embrace, laughing eyes glittering, and smiling lips dropped a kiss on first one corner and then the other of her trembling mouth. "Jamie," he growled, "you talk too much."

His teasing touch roved her face. When she would have spoken again, he stopped her words with the soft pressure of his kiss. Here, there, never lingering, he traced the contours of her cheek with his lips. Never did his kiss become more than a whisper. Never did the unfamiliar abrasiveness of his jaw more than brush hers. Jamie lay passively in his arms, accepting. His touch was gentle, his kiss pleasing, she told herself. Yet within her grew a strange dissatisfaction. A tiny fire flamed, spreading its warmth deep in her soul. Her pulse quickened, and her breathing lost its even rhythm. Of their own volition her lips parted beneath his. But he denied her submission and left unquenched a longing she had never known before.

His lips burned over her silken skin. Impatiently, lost and incomplete, her mouth sought his, and again he drew back with a husky chuckle. When her breath caught in her throat in a sad, tiny sigh, the hand that held her prisoner moved to her hip, drawing her closer. Then she knew his desire. Slowly, reluctantly, he moved away. Yet the pressure of his hand did not lessen. Tugging at a long, dark lock, he tilted back her head.

"Now do you understand?"

Jamie blushed, refusing to meet his gaze; perversely, silently she was denying a mutual desire that was undeniable.

"Stubborn little thing." The chuckle that rumbled in his chest was gently mocking. He drew her head back against his shoulder while he stroked the flowing strands of her hair. "Never mind. The day will come when you can't reject what's between us. Fight it as you will, my little one, it won't be denied. But enough for now. I have a surprise for you."

He set her from him and stood. She swayed unsteadily and would have fallen, but for his hand at her elbow. Mutely she followed him to the table where the candle burned low, flickering at the last of its strength. Mike pulled her chair from the table, indicating with a nod that she should be seated. From the one remaining carton he lifted a luscious meringue pie. A rakish smile played across his face as he cut and served her a generous slice.

"Oh, dear." She groaned. "You do know all my secrets. Lemon meringue pie is my favorite dessert."

"Then dig in." He watched delightedly as she began to eat. The look of absolute pleasure that crossed her face at the first bite drew an appreciative chuckle from him.

"Aren't you having any?" she asked, her fork poised in midair.

"It's more fun to watch you."

"Why?"

"I'd rather watch and wonder if this is how you'll look when I first make love to you."

Her fork fell from nerveless fingers with a clatter. "Why do you insist on saying such outrageous things? Can't you just leave it alone? I've known you a total of thirteen hours and all you've done is complicate my life."

"The word is complete."

"Complete? Complete what?"

"I complete your life, just as you complete mine."

"I," she stated emphatically, "have exactly nothing to do with your life, complete or otherwise."

"Yes, you do, Jamie. My life is your responsibility. You made it so when you—"

"Don't say it! Don't say, even one more time, that I saved your aggravating life. If you do, so help me, I'll find that can and stuff you in it. All seven feet of you."

"Only six two."

"Six two. Eight two. Who cares? A giant by any other name would be as annoying."

"You're fracturing famous quotes again."

"And you're fracturing my peace of mind."

"If you would just accept the truth, none of this would be upsetting you. It's a waste of time to fight what's meant to be. You might delay it a bit, but it will be the same in the end. We belong together."

"Never!"

"Yes. Yesterday, today, and tomorrow," he promised.

"Today might have brought me the disaster of meeting you. But with any luck tomorrow will be as untainted by your presence as yesterday."

Mike shook his head, looking at her in patient amusement. "When will you stop this useless fighting? Don't you know that all our yesterdays were spent in preparation for this day? Anything either of us has ever done was simply a prelude for this moment. Whatever fool hurt you, then let you go, played a significant role in bringing you to me. God! I'm sorry you were hurt, but I'm just as glad he let you go."

"Nobody really hurt me. I made a mistake." Jamie stared down at the remains of the pie before her, unable to meet his eyes, unwilling to let him see the unrest stirring in her.

"He was a fool." The low growl was curiously hoarse. Jamie looked up to find him watching her in grave concern.

"No, I was the fool. He was a kind man caught in an impossible situation." Her normally husky voice had dropped to no more than a whisper.

Mike covered her hand as it lay listlessly on the table. Slowly he lifted it and kissed the palm. His eyes never left hers. "Will you tell me about him?"

"It's not something I like to talk about."

"I can understand that." She tried to free her hand, but he would not allow it. With gentle pressure he clasped it tighter. His green gaze willed her to stop her struggles. "Jamie, tell me. Please."

"I can't. I have to clear the table." She started to rise.

"The table be damned!" In one swift move, he was on his feet and she had been swept into his arms. Before she could protest, he was striding to the sofa. There he settled her on his lap, his arms holding her close. "Now, tell me, so I can help."

"I can't," she whispered into his shirt.

"Yes, you can, Jamie. There's nothing you can't tell me." Gently he drew her head against his chest, then smoothed the tumbled locks. He waited and did not speak.

The quiet of the room was unbroken. Jamie was stubbornly determined to remain silent. She would not share her past with this stranger, she told herself.

"Start from the beginning, honey. It will hurt at first, but talking about it will ease the pain, I promise." His words were soft, but no less insistent.

Jamie sat tensely within the circle of his embrace. Gradually, without notice, she began to relax. Only a bit at first, then more as his hypnotic stroking of her hair continued. Perhaps it was the unfamiliarity of a comforting hand or the seductive warmth of his encircling arms. Whatever the reason, she began to speak without conscious thought. "I don't think I could explain without going back into my childhood. That's really when it all began."

"Then start there. I want to know it all."

"But it's such a long story."

"I have all night, Jamie." The words were spoken quietly into her hair. His lips remained there as he waited for her to resume.

"Mine is a big family. You already know that I have six older brothers. Not only am I the youngest, but no one else is under six feet. Even my mother is tall. We were rowdy and active, and a sports-oriented family. Each of us was involved in at least one sport. My oldest brother played professional football for a while, one plays tennis, another golf. My favorite brother coaches at the local high school. All my life I've lived with football, basketball, golf, or tennis. Naturally I wanted to be an athlete too. To state the obvious I'm too short for basketball. I do play tennis and swim, but my real love was gymnastics. I can't even tell you when I started; it just seems to be something I've always done. I trained long and hard, trying in my sport to measure up to my brothers in their sports. I did have my small share of success. When I was sixteen, I was considered a good prospect for the Olympics."

"Is that when you broke your arm?"

She nodded almost angrily. "It was a stupid, senseless accident. I tripped over a piece of broken concrete on a dark sidewalk."

"Because of that you missed the competition."

"Yes. My family was terribly disappointed, so for the next four years I worked harder than ever. I spent all my time practicing, working, competing."

"From sixteen to twenty you trained intensely. I can see how it would be necessary, but did you take the time for the normal teenage activities? Did you date, go to dances, or do any of the things a young girl enjoys?"

A bitter laugh accompanied an abrupt shake of her head. "You forget, if I wasn't working, I was competing. There was no time for the so-called normal activities."

"Did you never date?"

"Never. At least not until David."

"Another gymnast?"

"No," she turned her eyes away from him absently, lost in her thoughts of the past. "He had been. He had even won the bronze at the Olympics, but when I met him, he had turned to coaching."

"Was he your coach?" Mike's hand gently massaged the tight tendons in her neck, sending a warmth through her that relaxed and comforted.

"For a while."

"What was he like?"

"Young, more innovative, handsome." Memories assaulted her, as she relived in her mind the days when they had been the golden couple. Jamie and David: bright, beautiful, and together they were going to conquer the world. She could remember the first time she saw him as if it were only yesterday.

Following her usual routine, Jamie worked out each day on the balance beam. She worked well alone, but she missed George. He had been a part of her life since she had been a skinny kid just learning to tumble. Now he was gone, forced into retirement by a heart attack. Today she would meet her new coach and she was distinctly nervous. She had heard of him, knew he was much younger, but beyond that she knew little.

A quiet hush had fallen over the gym before she knew he was there. All the other girls staring raptly at the door was her first inkling that a stranger was in their midst. Slowly Jamie followed the path of their gazes and found herself looking into the most beautiful gray eyes she had ever seen.

He was not tall, but his body was so perfectly proportioned that he was an artist's dream. Blond and handsome, he smiled at her and she felt the first stirrings of feminine response. All the things she had never known, nor needed, as a young girl were sparked into life. For the first time Jamie felt like a woman, with a woman's desire for masculine attention. It was the beginning, a time of enchantment.

They become a team. The skills of one blending and meshing with those of the other. Enhancing and improving at every turn. Equally as compatible in their personal lives, they drifted into a deep friendship. After the long, hard hours of the training sessions there would be a quiet time of relaxing together. Shared laughter and kind encouragement made the work worthwhile. Both on the circuit and off, they were, indeed, the golden couple. Together they were invincible and Jamie had a string of victories to prove it. The ultimate dream was nearly hers.

Each victory brought it closer, and the elation grew. In the final competition Jamie was the girl to beat. Her scores were the best, her performance nearly flawless, and David was with her every step of the way. On the eve of the final competition, caught in the mad euphoria of victory, passion flamed like a wild thing. With student leading teacher, guiding even as she learned, they made love. And Jamie was certain she knew her destiny. David and the Olympics would be hers. She was happy as she had never been before. But the happiness was doomed to be short-lived, and tragedy lurked in the shadows.

On the last day of the competition it was a foregone conclusion that Jamie would win. She had been in top form, her performance the best yet. Then in the middle of a perfect execution, through one of those inexplicable flukes of chance, her foot slipped and Jamie fell. As she sat in the horrified hush that had fallen over the arena, clutching a bleeding, shattered ankle, no one had to tell her that a dream had shattered as well.

Her convalescence was slow. With a steel pin and therapy she was assured she would eventually walk without a limp, but the flexibility would be gone, and with it the consuming passion of her life. Gymnastics would forever be a thing of the past. Her one goal, the concentration of all her energies, had been swept out of reach by a split-second miscalculation. It was a knowledge so painful that it made the agony of her ankle negligible.

To his credit David was her faithful attendant. Not a day passed that he was not by her side, encouraging and promising that nothing had changed. But Jamie knew better. Without the cohesiveness of a common interest there was a strain between them that grew, eating away at what they had known like a greedy monster. They became more and more uncomfortable together. They drew further and further apart until at last Jamie sent him away.

The tears she had shed then had not been for a lost love, but for love that had never been. She had cried quietly and privately for a friendship that might have endured, but for the impetuous infatuation of a naive girl.

Mike's hand at her cheek brought her back to the present. His thumb brushed away her tears. For a time she had forgotten the last six years and the man who was holding her now. It was not until he murmured soothing words that she realized she had been speaking aloud.

"Don't be afraid, darling. It will be different this time. I know you've never trusted any man since, but I can change all that."

"No. It's not men that I don't trust. It's myself, my own judgment. I've mistaken infatuation for love once. I've never wanted to take the risk again," she spoke softly. "Because of the life I've led, I'm ill-equipped for the war between the sexes."

"It doesn't have to be war. It can be beautiful, I promise. Let me teach you."

Lulled by the seductive tone of his words, Jamie was suddenly and acutely aware of his masculinity. Throughout her revelation, she had been unaware of everything except the warmth and comfort he was offering. Now she was achingly conscious of a thousand things. The way his hair curled over his ears, then swept back in a slight wave. The slight crook of his brow as he gave her a quizzical smile. The half-moon scar at the right corner of his lips. The breadth of his chest and the overwhelming strength of his arms that made her feel cared for and protected. But most of all she felt a powerful need to sink into the circle of his embrace and surrender all that he might ask.

"Oh, no!" She jerked herself from his grasp, and in one strong bound was beyond his reach.

"Jamie." Mike's need to take her back into his arms was an almost tangible thing, but reason commanded that he should not act on it. She had shared her hurt, and it was a beginning. The first crack in the shell she had built around herself had begun, and he vowed to use any method, be it fair or foul, to tear it away completely. "I won't hurt you, you have my promise. And whether you admit it or not, over the last six years you've grown up. Your convalescence, the year you spent as an exchange student, then the four years you hid, teaching in that elite French school—all that has served the purpose. You're older and wiser. You won't make the same mistake again."

"Thank you for your vote of confidence. you must be a genius. On the strength of a few hours acquaintance you've decided you know me better than I know myself. I salute you for your great astuteness, but if you don't mind, I've had enough for one day." The bitter words were filled with emotional fatigue. The lines of her tense body spoke of a deep-seated weariness that only a mind in turmoil could produce.

"All right, Jamie. I'll go, but I'm not giving up. You need me more than you know. One day you'll realize it, and I'll be here. I promise."

Jamie turned away and did not hear when he quietly left the room.

Chapter Three

The sun was barely rising above the horizon when Jamie turned her small, dependable Volkswagen into the second-floor entrance of the parking deck. To her consternation her space was occupied. Not by another car, as sometimes happened, but by a grinning green-eyed giant.

He was lounging against the concrete railing that divided this section from that of another rental space. Anger flushed Jamie's cheeks a becoming peach. This was exactly what she had hoped to avoid when she had left her unrestful bed an hour earlier than usual. Efficiently she parked the car. The slam of its small door forecasted her mood before she spoke.

" 'Morning, Jamie." He forestalled the storm with his cheerful greeting, but only for the space of her exasperated sigh.

"I had hoped it might be a good morning, or at least an improvement over yesterday, but now I can see I was vastly mistaken. What are you doing here at this time of day? Yesterday it was over an hour later."

"Ah-ha! Just as I thought. You deliberately came early to avoid me."

"That's not true. I have extra work to do, thanks to you."

"Then you wanted to see me?"

"Certainly not!"

"Then you *were* avoiding me."

"Certainly not." A telltale blush gave the more truthful answer.

"Jamie." A large hand cupped her chin to raise her face to his.

"What?" she snapped.

"You're fibbing. Both times."

"That statement is not only ridiculous, it's utterly impossible. How could I want to avoid you and see you at the same time?"

"Simple. Your head says no to me, but your heart says yes. You aren't fighting me, Jamie. You're fighting yourself." He scorched her with a penetrating look. "That lovely body of yours is about to become a battlefield. It's going to be interesting to watch. Sort of like reading a book when you already know the end. Predictable, but interesting anyway."

"Must you always speak in riddles?"

"No riddle, honey. I'm going to give you all the time you need and let you struggle all you want, but the outcome will be the same. I'm yours, and avoid me as you will, you are mine. But"——his voice dropped to a conspiratorial whisper—"you know that already, don't you?"

"Certainly not! You . . . you . . ." she sputtered in complete frustration.

"You got out of bed too early this morning. You sound like a broken record." He took her briefcase from her. "Better come along. If we dawdle, the crowds will be arriving."

Defeated by his logic, Jamie let him lead her down the incline to the sidewalk. As yesterday the street was deserted. Bill could be heard farther down the block. The cans, as he rousted them back and forth, rang hollowly in the cavelike corridors formed by the tall buildings.

Walking in determined silence, Jamie would have passed by the window filled with swimsuits that only yesterday she had stopped to admire. It was his hand on her arm that stopped her.

"That's a sexy suit." With a nod he indicated the brilliant red bikini that could be crumpled and hidden from sight within even her small palm. "You'd look terrific in it."

"I'd get arrested in it."

"Lucky cop." He grinned.

"Are you never serious?" She turned sharply to continue her walk to the Bradford Building.

"You know I can be very serious." His fingers at her elbow as much as his words brought back the memory of the kisses they had shared. Jamie tried quietly to extricate herself from his hold. He only smiled and guided her across the street.

"Did you like it?" His voice cut across her reverie.

"Did I like what?" She slanted a glance at his innocent face. Had he read her thoughts? Could he know that her lips still burned with the memory of his touch?

"Why, the bikini, of course. Whatever else could I mean, Jamie?" A slow, lazy grin spread over his face as he began to whistle a low, haunting love song.

At the steps of the Bradford Building he stopped. "I won't come any further with you. I have an early appointment with a realtor. Gotta rush if I'm to be on time. Have a good day, love, and I'll see you tonight. Same time, same place." He dropped a kiss on the tip of her nose and walked rapidly away.

"But I . . ." In frustration she watched his retreating back. Why did she feel as if she had been hit by a tank? How was she going to cope with this annoying man who refused to take no for an answer?

"Hello, Miss Brent," the security guard greeted cheerfully.

"Hello, Mr. Hanson."

"It's a beautiful day, isn't it?"

"Yes"—her voice sank to a low mutter—"if you call it beautiful to be accosted by a giant, then I guess it's a beautiful day."

"I beg your pardon?"

"Nothing, Mr. Hanson. I was just thinking aloud. Excuse me. Now that I've gotten rid of my Chinese friend, I'd better get to work."

The puzzled security guard watched her trim figure until she stepped into the elevator. "Strange girl, but mighty pretty though," he said to the empty lobby.

Because of her training Jamie moved with an artless grace. No one would have gussed that her knee was aching with a dull pain. Her only concession to her injury was in the way she had dressed. Today she wore slacks to hide the unsightly blotch on her leg. Thankful that the hallway was still empty, she made her way to her office. Soon the working day would start, then hopefully she would be able to block the memory of burning kisses from her mind. Work! That was the answer. Grimly she immersed herself in the tasks she had set for the day.

"Boy, aren't you the busy beaver?" Meg's pixie face peered at her from the open door. "I knocked twice, but you didn't hear. You've been working nonstop for hours. Take a break."

"Come on in, Meg, I do need a rest. Mmm, coffee. I need that too." Jamie gratefully accepted the cardboard cup that held the steaming black liquid. She sipped it gingerly. "Sit down, Meg. Don't hover."

"How's your raspberry? Does it hurt?" The redhaired girl sank into the chair opposite Jamie.

"My *strawberry's* fine. My knee is a little stiff, but it's not really painful."

"Uh, Jamie, have you read today's paper?"

"No. I left too early this morning to even scan it."

"Then I think maybe you'd better read this." Meg handed a battered newspaper over the desk.

" 'An oil slick was spotted off the coast of North Carolina yesterday.' " Jamie read aloud. " 'A Navy pilot—' "

"No, no, not that. Read Suzy Sanderson's 'About Town.' "

"Meg, I don't read gossip columns. They never

have anything to say that interests me," Jamie protested.

"I think you'd better make an exception this time. Read the section circled in red. I found this in the lounge when I went for my coffee break. I don't know whose paper it is, but I think it's safe to assume it was there for a purpose. Read it, Jamie," Meg urged. "You need to."

"All right, if you insist, but I stil—" Jamie gasped as her eyes focused on the circled words. She began to read aloud, her expression stunned. " 'Will the handsome, dashing, and heretofore elusive young millionaire, John Bradford, be hearing wedding bells? He has been seen about town with a beautiful former Olympic hopeful. Is she friend, fiancée, or lover? One reporter who asked nearly lost his head. Is the dashing man so protective of the lady because she is, or because she isn't? Is or isn't what? That remains the question. Only time will tell. In the meantime our no-longer-so-elusive bachelor seems truly smitten. Ah! Young love.' " The paper crumpled in Jamie's hands as she glared down at it.

"I'm sorry, Jamie. I thought you should know. Can you imagine the field day the office gossips will have with this?"

"But why would anyone want to print such drivel? There's not a grain of truth in it. Seen about town indeed! Yesterday morning was the first time I'd ever seen the man in my life."

"You're going to have to face it: John Bradford is news. Everything he does makes the papers. Maybe that's why he tries to stay out of the public eye as much as possible. Suzy dubbed him 'the elusive reclusive' a long time ago. Poor guy, he must feel like he lives in a fishbowl."

"John Bradford? His name *is* John Michael Bradford, but surely he's not—" At Meg's affirmative nod Jamie stammered on. "But when I asked, he said he didn't work in this building."

"He doesn't. Actually he owns it."

"Oh, no!" Jamie moaned. "And I called him a lunatic."

"Ouch."

"Meg, I've never seen him around here before. Surely if he was that—" Jamie paused and brightened as a new thought occurred. "Maybe he's a wealthy relative and the Bradfords just happen to be fond of the name John."

She had put forth the idea hopefully, then at Meg's shake of her head knew she was grasping at straws. "Then why haven't I seen him around here before, for heaven's sake?"

"You haven't seen him," Meg said patiently, "because he does a great deal of the traveling for the company. Recently he's been integrating several small French companies with his. That's why we need a translator and why you have this job, Jamie."

"But you didn't see him! Maybe . . ." Jamie gave her argument one more futile try.

"No, Jamie. Your John Bradford is the one and only."

"He's not *my* John Bradford!" The irritation she had tried to control all morning rose to the surface and Jamie no longer cared who he might be.

"Tell Suzy Sanderson that."

"I intend to. That and a lot more. Do you realize she hinted I was his mistress? Good grief! What will people think? What will my family think? My brothers!"

"I've always envied you that half a dozen handsome men, but somehow not today. What can you do?"

"I could sue."

"You know that won't work. If there's anyone who's in doubt about your identity, that would confirm it. Anyway, the article doesn't mention your name. The town's full of beautiful women who'd like a chance at him. Suzy could have meant anyone."

"Sure there are," Jamie drawled disgustedly. "And how many former Olympic hopefuls are there?"

"Good point," Meg admitted. "But I still don't think you should dignify the article by answering in any way. What I can't understand is how the papers got hold of all this in the first place."

"There was some sort of tip. Mike says he'll know who's responsible by this afternoon."

"Mike?" Meg's brows arched over curious brown eyes.

"Mr. Bradford, then."

"If you hadn't read the paper, how did you know there'd been any contact with the reporters?"

"Meg, you'd have to have seen it with your own eyes to believe what happened to me yesterday. It was all so ridiculous that even I can't believe it happened." Jamie related the events of the evening before succinctly, leaving out only the kisses she had shared with Mike. Meg listened quietly, her eyes incredulous. Only her occasional "Wow" or "Gosh" punctuated Jamie's narrative.

When Jamie finished, neither woman spoke for long minutes. Jamie was reliving the memories of the part of the evening she had left untold, while Meg was speechless with surprise.

"Jamie," Meg cleared her throat and ventured cautiously, "are you sure he told the reporters you were his fiancée?"

"Of course, I'm sure. It's not exactly the sort of thing I'd be mistaken about, is it?"

"No, I guess not," Meg mused. "Golly! Do you know what this means?"

"Sure, for a few days we'll be a seven-day's wonder. Then all the interest will die down as if it had never happened."

"No." Meg shook her head. "I don't think so."

"Why ever not?" Jamie exploded.

"Well, John Bradford, uh, Mike himself is the reason. Haven't you wondered why you haven't at least seen a picture of him?"

"Not really." Jamie shrugged. "I suppose it's because he guards his privacy too much to allow photographs."

"Exactly! He's a very private person. No one but his closest friends ever know in advance what he's doing and where he is. That kind of secrecy drives the press crazy. What they don't know, they speculate about."

"Tell me about it," Jamie drawled sarcastically.

"Don't you see, Jamie? Yesterday Mike himself

handed out some news about his private life. That's so intriguing the press will be violently curious."

"Don't you think *violently* is a rather strong word?"

"I wish it were. This engagement, or love affair, is going to be the topic of conversation for a long time to come, I'm afraid."

"This is worse than ridiculous. Mike said that only because a terrible reporter had the nerve to ask if I was his lover."

"And he shielded you with a lie. Or is it a lie? Maybe he'd like it to be the truth."

"Meg! What was in your coffee? It's a little early to be hitting the bottle, don't you think?"

"Now, wait a minute, Jamie. Don't shrug this off. For a man like your Mike to open up to the press, there must've been a powerful reason. He could easily have told them something else. No, I think he had a reason for saying you were his fiancée."

"Now I know you're drunk. I only met him yesterday—and he's not *my* Mike!"

"How long does it take? Couldn't one day be enough to fall in love? Who decides how long it should take?"

"That's exactly what he said," Jamie murmured, a thoughtful look stealing across her face.

"Said what?" Meg watched her friend curiously. "Jamie? Jamie?"

"Oh, sorry, Meg. I was thinking."

"Yeah, sure." Meg rose from her seat. "I'd better get back to work if I want to keep my job." She moved to the door, then paused to turn back to Jamie. "And he just scooped you up in his arms in front of all those reporters?"

Jamie only nodded in answer.

"Wow!" The door closed behind Meg, leaving her friend to ponder all she had said.

Spinning her chair away from her desk, Jamie sat for a long while staring out the window, her thoughts again on the day before. He had a penchant for taking her up into his arms. How many times had he held her? Five? Six? Jamie knew she was kidding herself. She knew how many times he'd held her. She remembered, too clearly, every time.

The ringing of the telephone at her elbow interrupted her memories. With a confused shrug of her shoulders she spun back to her desk and lifted the receiver. "Jamie Brent's office."

"May I speak with Miss Brent, please?"

"Speaking."

"Good morning, Miss Brent. This is Suzy Sanderson."

"I have nothing to say to you, Miss Sanderson." Jamie's low voice was far more controlled than she felt.

"Surely you'd like to set the record straight. After all, there were some pretty personal questions asked yesterday. People are wondering about the true nature of your relationship with the glamorous Mr. Bradford."

"Thanks to you."

"Come now, Miss Brent, you can't blame me for printing the facts."

"You don't know the facts, Miss Sanderson."

"Would you care to elaborate on that a bit more?" Avid curiosity pulsated in the question.

"No, I would not." Jamie very gently replaced the receiver, then immediately lifted it again, viciously punching the intercom button.

"Meg, can you watch my office for me? I'd like to take the rest of the day off. I've some thinking to do. Are you sure you don't mind? Thanks. You're a life saver."

For the next few hours Jamie wandered the city. She stopped by the library to check on the books she had been waiting for. Perhaps it was just as well her wait was not yet over. Today, with all its turmoil, was definitely not the time to begin a suspenseful best seller. The museum, usually one of her favorite places, held no magic for her. In desperation she visited the zoo, certain the antics of the animals would prove a diversion. Once more a tried and true pleasure was without its usual zest.

At six o'clock, with an empty stomach and a stiff knee, a weary Jamie made her way home. She had deliberately chosen this time, hoping to thwart any persistent reporters. With relief she saw that no one was lurking outside her apartment building or in the lobby. Safe! Now all she had to contend with was the annoying, determined, and frankly devastating John Michael Bradford. Mike.

Jamie stepped from the elevator and walked to her apartment door, her step light, an impish grin curving her lips. She had, in a sudden inspiration, decided how the remainder of the evening would be conducted. The jolly green-eyed giant was in for a surprise!

Because her knee would benefit from the heat, she

soaked in the tub longer than usual. After drying, smoothing on a scented lotion, and brushing the damp tendrils of dark hair from her face, she rummaged deep into the back of her closet. A chuckle of satisfaction bubbled in her throat as she drew out the oldest pair of jeans she owned.

Years ago they had been her favorites, as evidenced by the frayed hems and the faded, soft patina found only in ancient denim. Even deeper in the closet's recesses she found hanging under an old flannel shirt the red sweatshirt she wanted. At least it had been red at one time. Now, after many washings, it was a particularly disgusting shade of pinkish orange. Her lucky rabbit's foot of days long gone still dangled from its zipper.

The chuckle had grown into a giggle by the time Jamie had loosened the towel tucked at her breasts. Wearing only the whisper-soft fragrance of the scented lotion, she walked to the open drawer that was filled with frothy, lacy underwear. Wickedly she extracted a pair of silk panties that were sinfully brief. Dancing to the mirror, she studied her firm, small bosom in the silvery glass. Striking a theatrical pose, she spoke to her reflection.

"To bra or not to bra. That is the question. Ha! That, Jamie me girl"—she leered at herself—"is a ridiculous question. Considering the way Mike Bradford looks at you with those green eyes, a corset wouldn't be a bad idea." One dancing turn and she was pulling the matching bra from the drawer.

A quick application of antiseptic cream to her now pain-free knee, a fresh Band-Aid, and she was ready to don her costume. She slid into the jeans, sighing in pleasure at their comfort. Next the sweatshirt slipped over her head. Not bothering with makeup other than a little lip gloss, she tackled her hair. The dampness of the tub had brought out hated natural curl.

Jamie brushed the mass relentlessly for a few minutes. Then deftly pulled it back and up. Three quick twists and most of the curl was hidden. Four bone pins anchored it to the crown of her head. She eyed herself critically in the mirror and liked what she saw. With a wink and a satisfied pat to the topknot, she turned to scrabble under the bed for her favorite pair of sneakers. These she withdrew with a happy smile, sparing only one sad cluck over the newest hole in the toe.

"Now, Jamie, my beauty." She turned back and forth, admiring her reflection, laughing anew at the patch at the seat of her pants. "You're guaranteed *not* to be what the dashing man-about-town wants. One look and he'll forget he ever had the slightest interest in you. Exit one Mike Bradford."

The chiming of the doorbell broke into her gleeful monologue. Her steps were again more dancing than walking as she moved gaily to the summons. She paused a second before opening the door, forcing her face into solemn lines, but nothing could hide the sparkle of laughter in her eyes. Eager for the battle, she flung the door wide.

"Ooooh, rats!"

"Not rats, honey. Only me." He stood in the doorway. Big, broad, handsomer than a mere mortal had the right to be, Jamie thought—and dressed in the most disreputable pair of jeans she had ever seen. His sweatshirt, once a deep navy blue, was now faded to a gorgeous shade of putrid purple. The tennis shoes he wore had no holes, but the laces had been broken and repaired with bits of laces of another color.

Jamie could only stand and stare. He was a magnificent satyr. Where was the debonair executive of yesterday and this morning? Never in her wildest dreams would she have pictured him as the man standing before her. He waited patiently while she mastered her astonishment. Silently, as yet unable to speak, she gestured him in.

"You look terrific, love. There's nothing I admire more than a woman with a sense of style." He kissed her brow softly as he passed by her. With loose-limbed grace he sank down onto the sofa, his green gaze indeed making her feel the need for the armor of a corset. "Come here. Sit by me and tell me about your day."

"Well, it wasn't a very good one." Even to Jamie the words were petulant. She knew her annoyance at being bested at her own prank was surfacing.

"Then come tell me about it. Maybe I can help."

"How can you help when you're the problem?" She sat down by his side, but some distance away.

"How am I the problem?"

"How are you the problem! Haven't you read the papers? Suzy Sanderson's column, to be specific."

"Oh, that." He shrugged.

"What do you mean, 'oh, that'? Didn't you read what she wrote?"

"Sure. But I didn't see anything to get upset about."

"I don't believe what I'm hearing. Aren't you the 'elusive reclusive'? The man who hates for the press to write about what he's doing, and with whom?"

"That has been true in the past," he agreed mildly.

"But not now?"

"Nope."

"And what, pray tell, is the difference?" Jamie fairly shrieked. "Why shouldn't you care what's written about you now?"

"It's simple. I don't care if the whole world knows about us."

"There is no us."

"Tell Suzy that."

"I intend to."

"She won't believe you, Midge."

"Oh, yes, she will, and don't call me Midge."

"She already suspects that you're, to use that archaic term again, my mistress."

"And by the time she's through hinting, everyone else is going to think so too, dammit."

"I could always make an honest woman of you. We could be married before the end of next week." Mike suggested, a hopeful look on his face.

"Never!"

"Never is a long time."

"Not long enough, believe me!"

"Jamie." The teasing tone had gone from his voice; he had grown quite serious. "I'm sorry about that article. The last thing I would ever want is for you to be uncomfortable or unhappy. I've already spoken with

Suzy. She's promised there'll be no more sly little innuendos about our relationship. From now on she'll print
only the facts."

"What facts are there to be printed?"

"Oh, you know, the usual tidbits seen in gossip
columns. That we were seen dancing into the wee
hours of the morning, or walking hand in hand in the
park, or even that you were my mother's houseguest
over the weekend. That sort of thing."

"We haven't done any of those things."

"I know, but we will. It's just a matter of time.
Anyway, we have to do something so Suzy can print it.
I promised."

"Wait. I must have missed something here. You
promised who what?"

"I promised Suzy that if she would lay off you, she
could have an exclusive."

"I'm sure I don't really want to know, but I'll ask.
What exclusive?"

"Why, a step-by-step account of our romance, of
course." Mike's look of amazement was a trifle over-
done, but Jamie's rage was not.

"You didn't . . . you couldn't . . . you wouldn't . . ."
she sputtered impotently.

"Didn't, couldn't, wouldn't what?" he asked innocently.

"Let that busybody think we're having an affair!"

"Jamie, I said romance, not affair."

"Same thing."

"No, honey. An affair has no commitment, we do.
Anyway, Suzy knows we're secretly engaged. I prom-

ised she could be the one to print it when we go public."

"Commitment! You should be committ*ed*. You're
crazier than I thought, and this is only day number two
of this insane relationship."

"You're counting the days, how wonderful. I feel
the same way. Except I count the seconds."

"And no one," Jamie continued, ignoring his grinning interruption, "could be so stupid as to think there
could be anything between us. Only an idiot would become engaged on such short acquaintance. You can bet
your bottom dollar that that woman thinks you said it
to cover up a sordid relationship. Now she's going to
be positive we're lovers. I might as well paint a scarlet
A across my forehead."

"Poor Jamie." Mike shook his head in mock sym-
pathy. "I did tell you I'd make an honest woman of
you."

"I wouldn't marry you if you were the last man on
the face of the city. You unmitigated—"

"Nincompoop," Mike offered.

"Yes, nincompoop. Thank you."

"You're welcome, and Jamie, you're fracturing
proverbs again. It's earth, not city. The last man on the
face of the earth, and that's really what I am as far as
you're concerned."

"That's exactly what I said."

"I know, but somehow I don't think we mean
quite the same thing." Mike's grin was delightedly
amused. "Jamie?"

"What now?" She braced herself for more.

"I'm hungry. Let's eat."

"I don't believe you! Right in the middle of my ruined reputation, you're hungry."

"It wasn't a proverb, but you surely fractured that sentence, and I'm worse than hungry. I'm starving. Can't we declare a truce and go? We do have an open reservation, but I'd like to get there before too late."

"Reservations? Dinner reservations?"

"Sure, what else?"

"Have you not noticed how I'm dressed?"

"I like how you're dressed. I especially like that patch on your, uh, on the back of your jeans. Red gingham with blue and yellow flowers was a stroke of sheer genius. Makes for a much more interesting—"

"Forget it! I can't go anywhere dressed like this, and anyway, I don't think we can have a truce."

"To have a truce all we have to do is agree not to quarrel for the rest of the night. Come on, let's shake on it." He extended his hand toward her and waited. "Jamie, please."

"Oh, all right." She couldn't keep the small smile that hovered on her lips hidden any longer as she placed her hand in his. "I'm beginning to see why you are so successful. You never lose, do you?"

"Not in the things that really matter to me," he murmured, no longer teasing. His eyes met hers and held them a long, unnerving moment. Before she could tear her gaze from his, a revealing blush crept over her face.

Moving swiftly, Mike stood and pulled her to her feet. "Get your keys and let's go. I'm getting hungrier by the minute, woman."

"Mike"—she tried one more time—"I can't go out like this."

"Yes, you can. There's only one thing wrong with the way you look." He stepped closer, his hand lifting to her hair. Skillfully and gently he plucked the bone pins from the top knot. As the hair cascaded down her back, he combed it with his fingers. He stroked and smoothed the shining curls into some semblance of order. "There. Now you're perfect."

"Sure I am. So when you want to be near perfect, just stand close to me," she teased with a flashing grin, wrinkling her pert nose.

"I have every intention of standing close. Very close."

"Trite joke," Jamie muttered, silently annoyed with herself for again falling into one of his traps.

His hands stopped their stroking and untangled from her hair to frame her face. Slowly his head descended to hers. There was no urgency, no deep, frantic need, only the sweet kiss of promise. When he lifted his lips from hers, Jamie could only think of this moment, this instant. There were no frustrations, no anger, no troublesome reporters, and no disillusioning mistakes in the past. There was only Mike.

Because of her intense training schedule, Jamie had never learned to hide her response behind a cloak of flirtatiousness. Those teen years when most girls were perfecting the art, she had spent perfecting her gymnastics skills. She had never been anything but straightforward and totally honest. That beguiling truthfulness was a window to her heart.

She feared the experienced man who was now

towering over her could read every thought that was sure to be written on her expressive face. Even now he was watching her silently, holding her gently, as she ran the gamut from elation to panic. Despite her efforts at control, her delicate brows arched up in wonder, her sapphire eyes sparkled in excitement, the soft and tender curve of her lips trembled on the brink of a smile. Then, just as swiftly, the smile faded, even as it was born. A shiver passed through her as a shutter came down over the glow in her face. Instantly her guard was up. She could feel his piercing gaze as she struggled valiantly to gather her scattered thoughts, to become again the coolly aloof Jamie. Jamie, who cloaked herself in aloneness. Now she felt the small crack that had appeared in her wall of defense, and she must begin to mend it, while she still could. The battle he had predicted had begun, and Jamie knew she was fighting herself as well as Mike.

Wisely he put her from him. The faintly mocking smile that marked his face was for himself, not the sweet innocent who could devastate him with her eyes. When he spoke, there was no mockery or teasing, only gentle caring.

"Tonight, whether you admit it or not, that shield you've been hiding behind has cracked. I serve you fair warning: I'll use any means to keep the rift open until someday you help me tear it away."

"I won't."

"You will, but don't be frightened. I might not be fair, but I will be gentle, I will be patient, and I will win." He touched her cheek softly, his voice even huskier. "I've never before been a patient lover, but never before was there a Jamie Brent."

"This is impossible," she whispered.

"No, honey, it's inevitable."

Jamie shivered beneath his certainty. With her once gleaming eyes grown dark, she reached for the pins that had held her hair. She felt the need to control the tangled locks as she would her capricious emotions.

"No," he growled, capturing her hand in his as it hovered over the low table where he had dropped the pins. "Leave it down. I like it free."

"Very well, if you wish." She could feel his anger at her need to withdraw behind her wall of total control for it grated in his voice. With stilted gestures she used her free hand to push her hair back from her shoulders. It fell gloriously, shining and healthy, to her waist. "If you still insist we go out to dinner dressed as we are, I suggest we leave now."

"Jamie"—he caught her other hand—"don't shut me out. The woman who opened the door to me tonight was alive and full of joy. Don't lock her away. She'll die, honey. She'll die without ever having lived. Let her be free and as vibrantly alive as she can be. Don't twist all your emotions into a tight little knot until they wither and die." He wound a strand of hair around his hand. "Don't confine her hair, or her spirit. Be a woman. Entrance me, beguile me, tease me as you did tonight with those marvelous clothes. For a moment I saw a woman who could conquer the world with her smile.

"Come out from behind that protective cloak that has kept you an innocent." He paused at the harsh hiss of her indrawn breath. "No, don't deny it. In many ways you're the most innocent twenty-six-year-old woman I've ever seen. Innocent in the ways of women, innocent of your strength. Come into the real world, stand on your own two feet, ply your womanly wiles. Flaunt your charms, flex your wings, and learn the power you can wield. Jamie, Jamie, you could drive a man to the brink of madness."

"You're crazy. I can't do that. I wouldn't know how."

"Then learn, and begin with me. First, last, and always."

She watched his solemn face for a long while. "You're serious, aren't you?"

"Never more."

"I don't understand. Why should you bother? Why should you care?"

"It's simple. I want you to come to me as all the woman you can be. I want the fire and I want the excitement only you can give me. Ours could be an explosive relationship. We could share a matchless love, but only if each of us brings total commitment to our joining. I'm selfish, honey; I want it all. I want the woman in my life to love me without reservations—as I'll love her."

"Mike, you're going too fast for me. All the other was fun and games compared to this. I'm not ready for it. I'm not sure I'll ever be."

"I hadn't intended getting into this tonight. You're right, it's far too soon. Let's forget it for now. I'm still starved."

Jamie burst into hearty laughter that was tinged with relief. "I suppose giants do need to refuel with a certain regularity. Come, you poor man, let's go."

Though an easy rapport had been established, she was still wary and was likely to be for some time. But the crack was still there in the wall. It was a beginning.

Chapter Four

 Mike and Jamie crossed the lobby under the watchful stare of Mrs. Horton. Her avid eyes did not miss the disreputable dress of either of them. A disdainful sniff resounded over the bridge table where she was playing cards with three other residents. With only the slightest pressure at Jamie's elbow, Mike guided her toward the watching women.

"Good evening, Mrs. Horton. Ladies." He bowed easily toward each. Smoothly and gracefully, he had become the gallant courtier, flashing a winsome smile at the stern-faced women. "It's good to see you again, Mrs. Horton. May I say how lovely you look this evening? That shade of lilac does wonders for your eyes. They're like violet pools. But forgive me, I'm forgetting my manners. Won't you please introduce me to your lovely companions?"

Jamie didn't hear what followed in his absurd performance. In her efforts to suppress the giggles that threatened to erupt, she lost the direction of the conversation. But she didn't miss the pretty pink blushes that, in turn, stained the faces of the four ladies. No one had to tell her that Mike was again bestowing outrageous and flamboyant compliments on the unsuspecting dowagers.

"If you beautiful ladies will excuse us"—his hand on her arm brought Jamie back into the conversation—"Jamie and I were just about to go out for a stroll." He wagged a teasing finger at them. "Now don't you worry. I'll take good care of her and have her home before too late."

The smile left his face and the look he turned on Jamie was filled with the care and concern of a man who loved deeply. She found she could only stare into the sparkling depths of his eyes, wondering if the invitation she saw in them was true. It was when he spoke solemnly and sincerely that she saw the mischief that lurked there. "Before we go, I'd like to thank you for keeping such a watchful eye on Jamie. I won't worry half so much when I'm away if I know all of you are taking such good care of her."

His fingers tightened on her arm to stop her strangled protest. He executed another courtly bow and turned up the voltage of his endearing smile. "Come along, darling. We've kept these good ladies from their game long enough. Good night, Mrs. Horton, Mrs. Price. Have a nice evening, Mrs. Washburn, Miss Adams." The latter was called over his shoulder as he virtually dragged a sputtering Jamie through the door.

In the questionable privacy of the street she could no longer hold back the laughter, and spasms of unholy glee shook her slender frame. Soon tears were coursing down her cheeks as she muttered remembered bits of his charade.

"A lovely shade of lilac, my foot. That was almost as hideously purple as your sweatshirt."

"Obviously she thinks it's lovely," he defended with an unrepentant grin.

"Violet pools indeed." This set off another gale of laughter.

"That was a nice touch, wasn't it?"

"Where's your hat?"

"What hat?" The smug smile slipped and a puzzled look replaced it.

"Why, your plumed hat, of course. The one that you should have swept grandly over the floor in your gallant act."

"Oh, *that* hat. It's out to the cleaners. I guess I've swept too many floors lately."

"You've an arsenal of charm, haven't you? You reach into your bag of tricks and pull out one that fits the occasion. The winsome 'aren't I cute?' little-boy smile is absurdly lethal. You had them all in the palm of your hand." Jamie chuckled.

"How about you? What does my winsome smile do to you?" He teased, but his eyes were serious.

Jamie cocked her head to one side in a dramatic pantomime of deep thought. "It's too soon to tell. Why don't you look me up when I'm their age and we'll see how susceptible I am?"

"I'll be around then, lady. You can bet on it." He took her arm as they began to stroll along the street.

After a few minutes of silence, Jamie spoke. "You do realize, don't you, that you've saddled me with four guardian angels? From now on I won't be able to make a move not recorded by their watchful eyes."

"Bless 'em. They have so little in their lives, why begrudge them the pleasure of seeing our romance develop?"

"We don't have a romance."

"We're going to."

"Don't start that again! If you do, I'm going to march right back upstairs. Then how are you going to explain to the peanut gallery about our short-lived romance?"

"Fine with me. The shorter the romance, the sooner we can get on to the good stuff." Mike lifted a brow suggestively.

"You are without a doubt the craziest, looniest, most—"

"Adorable idiot?"

"Yes, idiot. Thank you."

"That's not exactly the same, but you're welcome anyway." His hand enfolded hers, his grip warm and gentle. "We'd better get a move on. I've a very important promise to keep."

"What promise?" She eyed him suspiciously.

"I promised the ladies I'd try to fatten you up a bit. It seems the poor dears are concerned about how thin you are. They suspect you skip meals and don't eat as much as you should."

"Drat." Jamie groaned. "What do they do, go through my garbage?"

"Nothing so drastic. If you'd been listening when the ladies and I were talking, you would've learned they've been concerned about you for quite some time."

"Why should they be concerned about me?"

"Jamie, have you never considered what their lives are like? They sit there day after day, not able to do much. So they live vicariously through the lives of those around them. It was Miss Adams who thinks you don't eat enough. Mrs. Horton worries that you spend too much time alone. Of course, I promised to remedy both concerns."

Jamie slanted a perceptive look at him. "You weren't just conning them. You really wanted to brighten their lives, didn't you?"

"If I can"—he shrugged—"why not?"

"My, my, my. A con man with a heart. You are a rare bird."

"Terrific! You're beginning to recognize my sterling qualities."

"Be serious a minute, idiot. That was a very nice thing to do." Impulsively she grasped a lock of his hair and pulled his head down. Rising on tiptoe, she kissed his cheek quickly.

Mike stopped short. His hand shook slightly as he touched the place where her lips had rested. Though he tried to regain his joking manner, his voice was hoarse when he spoke. "Honey, if you'll keep doing that, I'll make a career out of finding little old ladies to cheer up."

Her light laughter filled the street as she ignored his barely hidden intensity. "You may have to make a career out of finding me. Where are we? I thought we were walking to your car. This looks like a park."

"It is. A friend of mine owns this land here in the heart of the city and he's turning it into a miniature park. It was his old family home. In fact, all the plants you see here have been planted at some time by his family." He steered her through a tall hedge and a wrought-iron gate.

"I grew up in this city, and I must have passed this hedge and fence thousands of times, never knowing how beautiful it was here."

"Not many people know about it. Actually the park has only been open a few days. It was the site of one of those old, elegant mansions that used to line this entire street before progress decreed the need for more skyscrapers and parking decks."

"I can remember," Jamie added, "when I was little, it made me sad to watch the houses being torn down. I hated the steel ball that battered them."

"Nate wouldn't let his house be torn down. He's turning it into an art gallery, and he's keeping the grounds as a minipark."

"Are we having dinner here?"

"You bet. You're about to have the most delicious, the most mouth-watering meal you could find."

"Hiya, Mike." A deep-throated shout came from beneath a red-and-white striped awning that covered a quaint hot dog stand. It nestled into the trees with flow-

ers surrounding it, a part of the beauty, not a distraction. "See ya brought the beautiful lady like you said."

The wizened old man smiled at Jamie with kind
eyes. "Glad you could come, Jamie. I'm Cholie."

She took the hand that he had thrust at her, surprised to find it callused and hard. "Hello, Charlie. I'm
glad I could come too."

"No, ma'am, not Charlie. It's Cholie." Jamie could
hardly believe such a sweet voice could come from so
rugged a man. "Now, how about one of my special
dogs? Made the chili fresh today when Mike said he
might be bringing you around."

"I'd love one, Cholie. I'm starved."

"Mike, take your lady over to a table by the lake.
I'll bring them over when they're ready."

"How about two of your special chocolate sodas
too?" Mike suggested.

"Comin' right up." Cholie flashed a grin and set to
work, whistling along with the music that seemed to be
floating through the trees.

Mike led Jamie to a small table at the water's edge.
When she was comfortably seated, he smiled and
pulled a small packet from the pocket of his pants.
"Can't sit by the lake and not feed the ducks."

"Where are they?"

"They'll be here, never fear. I think they hear me
coming before I leave the gate. Hopefully tonight we'll
finish our dinner before they attack."

"Attack? Isn't that rather a strong word for a duck?"

"You're in for a surprise. There's nothing meaner
than an impatient duck."

"Here it is, folks. Two of Cholie's special dogs. Eat and enjoy."

With a flourish Cholie set before them two of the most glorious hot dogs Jamie had ever seen. They were smothered with relish, coleslaw, and finally a dollop of thick, spicy chili. Next came sodas, rich and darkly chocolate, with whipped cream poised on top like a cloud. A brandied cherry trickled a rivulet of deep pink across the molded chocolate leaf beneath it.

"Marvelous." Jamie leaned back to stretch, and breathed deeply. It was the first time she had spoken since Cholie had placed the food before them. "I never dreamed I could eat so much, and the soda was pure heaven."

"Cholie will be pleased that you liked it. He claims making them is a lost art. After having one of his, I tend to agree."

"So do I."

"Uh-oh. Prepare to be invaded. Here come my little friends."

Jamie turned to follow Mike's nod. There, marching in single file along the lakeshore, were five of the fattest and most colorful ducks she had ever seen. Their feathers were iridescent in the soft light of the street lamps. With unswerving purpose they waddled toward the table, stopped before Mike, and waited expectantly.

"Watch," he whispered, looking across the lake, pretending not to see the gathering at his feet. One duck, the largest and most impressive, quacked softly. Mike ignored him. Once more the duck quacked, and added a slight nudge to Mike's foot. Still there was no response. With a flurry of ruffled feathers, the duck squawked furiously and pecked Mike's ankle.

"Ouch! Herman, that hurt." The words were scolding, but there was a smile on Mike's face as he opened the packet of bread crumbs. "Here, you greedy monsters. Eat this and then go away and leave me alone with my girl."

Laughing, Jamie asked for crumbs so she could join in the fun. She happily scattered the bread on the grass and laughed anew at the antics of Mike's feathered friends. Soon all the crumbs were gone.

"That's all, Herman. Take your squadron and go." The ducks stood, waiting. "You heard me. No more for you tonight. You're going to sink when you take your nightly swim if you get any fatter. Shoo! Scat!" He waved them away. With one last protest Herman led his brood back to the lake.

"Amazing. I could swear that duck understood you." Her words were punctuated by low musical chuckles.

"Of course, he understood me. Herman's a very intelligent bird." Mike took Jamie's hand and led her back to the table. Soon they had the papers and cups cleared away and deposited in the nearby trash holder.

"Thanks, Cholie," Mike yelled. "You still make the best dogs in the world."

"And don't forget the sodas," Jamie added. "It was a rare pleasure to meet you, Cholie."

"Same here, Jamie. Come back anytime. The next soda's on the house. See ya, Mike."

Mike and Jamie strolled around the lake. There were clusters of plants and evergreens scattered about in thoughtfully planned abandon. The atmosphere was one of natural beauty, but only because it had been carefully nurtured. Jamie did not protest when Mike's arm fell easily about her shoulders, his stride matching her shorter one. Walking in this fashion, they did not speak. There was no need.

From the first there had been few people in the park, but now it was virtually deserted. As they followed a winding path, even the music seemed to drift away. The terrain became rougher and the plants weren't as well tended, but they were beautiful nonetheless.

"This part of the park is the old family garden. Most people skip it, but it's my favorite. Some of the boxwoods here are older than either of us. In fact, considering the age of the house and the grounds, they could be almost a hundred years old."

"I didn't realize they could live so long." Jamie marveled at the shrubs.

"Sure they can. I can't tell you much about them, but Nate can, if you like."

"I'd love to hear more. I can't believe this place has been here all these years and I never knew."

"Nate's family were very private people. Only their closest friends were ever invited here."

"So why has he opened it to the public?"

"Nate's a maverick and never fit the family mold. He feels beauty is to be shared, not hidden away." Mike swept the area with a look of appreciation. "He's right, it is too beautiful to be secret." He looked at Jamie. "I love this place. That's why I wanted to share it with you."

"Thank you." There was nothing more she could say, her heart too full for more.

"Come," Mike murmured softly. "There's a special place I want to show you."

Hand in hand they left the pathway. He led the way, carefully holding branches back from her. There were briars and ivy growing over the trail in many places.

The full moon had risen, its light filtering through the trees, brightening their way almost as well as the lamps had before. Once Mike paused, but a gentle finger against her lips stopped her question. He pointed to a nearby tree branch. The big yellow eyes of an owl stared unblinkingly back at them. It did not seem frightened, but patiently waited.

With a slight squeeze of her hand, Mike indicated that they should move on. Jamie was aware of his strength and the hardness of his callused palm. A strange hand for one of the city's most successful executives, Jamie thought. Stranger still was the decidedly feminine ring he wore on the little finger of his left hand. It was a graceful, old-fashioned ring of sapphires and pearls, its setting antique gold. Perhaps, Jamie mused, it was a family heirloom of sentimental value. Still, why did he wear it fitted so tightly on his finger? What hautning memories did it hold? Why did he feel the need to keep it with him always?

Jamie couldn't remember when she had first noticed the ring. It was simply there. He wore it comfortably, with no excuses for its delicacy. Search her memory as she might, she could not visualize it on the hand that had gripped her ankle that fateful morning of their meeting. Had he worn it then? Or had it just appeared? What story could the ring tell of this man who, despite her protestations, intrigued her beyond measure? Several times this evening she had almost questioned him about it. Yet she found herself curiously reluctant. Had it belonged to a woman who meant a great deal to him? A sweetheart? A lover? And, she asked herself, why should she care? It had nothing to do with her. She shouldn't care . . . but she did.

"Jamie?"

"Sorry, my mind wandered for a second." She clasped his hand tighter as he guided her carefully over a fallen tree.

"I was saying that this part of the park is to be kept in its natural state. Nate hopes the local Scout troops will use it for nature studies. If we're quiet, we might see a wild animal or two. Maybe even a deer."

"You're kidding! Here in the heart of the city?"

"It's not so amazing. There are several hundred acres here that the city sort of grew around. The entire acreage is fenced and hedged. It's been the sanctuary for many animals for a long time. Nate admits that the deer were imported. But they're still very much the wild animals they always were. Within these grounds they can roam freely and more safely than in any forest."

"I still can't believe this place." Jamie's amazement was complete at this small haven beyond the city's streets.

He chuckled. "You'll get used to it after a while."

Stepping over stones and dodging low-hanging branches. Mike moved easily. With his right hand he continued to shield her from the enroaching limbs as he led her deeper into the shadows. His left hand held her gently. Abruptly he stopped and faced her. She lifted her eyes to his, a puzzled expression on her face.

"I have a surprise for you. Close your eyes and don't open them until I say." He did not whisper, but his words were low and hushed.

Jamie did as he asked. His hand grasped her shoulders as he guided her forward. "Don't cheat," he said. "Keep them closed tightly."

"I promise. No cheating." She smiled in the darkness at his boyish enthusiasm.

"We're almost there. Careful, a stone to your right. Good girl. You must've been a Girl Scout." With these encouragements and a constant verbal description of the terrain. Jamie was able to walk blindly, trustingly, where he led. Without warning she sensed a difference in the air. A light breeze caressed her face and she knew they had left the trees and were now in an open area. Mike stopped again and Jamie stood by him, waiting expectantly.

"You can open your eyes now, Jamie," he said softly in her ear. "We're here."

"Mike!" she could only whisper, "what a lovely place."

They were standing on a low-rising hill, and before them was a small clearing. A tiny lake, as blue as the sapphire of Mike's ring, nestled among the trees and low-growing plants. With a start Jamie realized it was a man-made lake. Ivy grew in profusion beside the flagstone walk, often encroaching and hiding the winding path. An arched footbridge of gray wood spanned from shore to a tiny island in the center of the sparklingly clear water. Verdant grass covered the islet, and at its very center stood a delicate gazebo.

"Would you like to go down?" His lips touched her hair as he spoke.

"Yes, please. I've never seen such a lovely place." Jamie started to move down the slight hill, but Mike's restraining hand at her arm halted her.

"Shhh, look." Jamie looked in the direction he indicated. There, poised at the edge of a group of trees, were three deer. Mike pulled her back against him, his arms winding about her waist. "If we're very still, perhaps they'll come drink from the lake."

He had whispered softly, his warm breath fanning her cheek. The very nearness of him sent a shiver of strange delight through her. Instinctively she relaxed against him.

"Are you cold?" He tightened his embrace.

"Not now." Her head rested beneath his heart, and she listened to the steady rhythm as she watched the graceful beauty of the wild animals below.

Hesitantly, with his head raised, the largest of the three stepped into the clearing. His nose searched the air for the scent of any threatening intruder. Since the light breeze had been nipping against her face, Jamie realized that he would not detect them. Breathlessly still, she waited in the shelter of Mike's arms as the smallest deer moved with caution into the clearing. A fawn scampered in her wake.

In single file, stepping daintily, the deer followed the worn trail to the water's edge. The fawn, growing brave, pranced now at his father's heels, strutting in comical imitation of his proud sire. Mike and Jamie laughed silently together as he gamboled ungracefully along.

The deer stood side by side, lowering their heads to drink. Often the buck would lift his head and scan the open field above them, constantly alert for danger.

From the trees behind them there was a sudden flurry of sound. The rustling of the trees preceded the flapping of the powerful wings of a night bird. With lightning speed the deer were off and running. With sure and graceful steps they bounded across the clearing and disappeared into the safety of the trees.

Quiet descended. Nothing moved in the moonlit clearing. The water was tranquil and the deer and owl might never have passed that way.

"Even if I pinch myself, I'm not sure I'm going to believe this."

"I'm glad we shared it, Jamie."

"So am I." She knew that it had been even more wondrous because she had shared it with him, and because his arms had held her as they watched.

"Are you ready to go down?"

"Sure."

"Race you," he challenged.

"You're on." With her laughter floating behind her Jamie charged down the hill and through the meadow. Fleet of foot, she ran like the deer.

Mike overtook her easily, though, pacing his stride to hers, neither falling behind nor drawing ahead. It was only as they neared the lake that he took the lead. At the shore he turned and waited.

Impish mischief danced in Jamie's eyes as she ran

full tilt at him. In self-defense he caught her in his arms, spinning her around with a carefree laugh.

"I won, now pay up," he commanded.

"We didn't have a bet."

"Doesn't matter. To the victor go the spoils."

"No fair. You cheated," Jamie protested.

"I did not cheat," he declared, still holding her in his arms.

"You only won because your legs are longer."

"Yours are prettier."

"I can see I'm not going to win this argument either." She sighed in mock exasperation. "Okay, I admit you won fair and square. You can put me down now."

"No."

"Why ever not?"

"Because you haven't paid me."

"You're a persistent rascal, aren't you?" Jamie grinned even as she wound her arms about his neck. She leaned forward to kiss his cheek, but instead found his lips met hers. The teasing kiss was little more than a fleeting touch, but their eyes met and held long after it had ended. Then slowly, Mike set her feet on the ground.

Jamie moved from him, needing to gather her scattered wits. She deliberately let herself fall beneath the spell of this magical place, taking its tranquillity for her own.

From the shore she could see the gazebo clearly. It was ancient and shabby. The delicately carved wood and lattices that formed a railing around it were rotted and in some places missing. The graceful pagoda roof, covered with slate shingles that were discolored with age, rose high to an elegant peak. Even in disrepair there was a lasting graciousness about the old derelict, its frailties adding to its charm. Now bathed in the light of a moonbeam, with faded, ancient wood glowing silver, the gazebo offered enchantment nestled among the ivy and moss.

Calmer, she faced him, and found his eyes devouring her. In an attempt to ignore his intensity, she asked lightly, "Can we go over to the island?"

"I'm not sure the bridge is safe. Since it isn't part of the public park, it's not as well cared for yet." At Jamie's crestfallen look he chuckled indulgently. "If you'll wait here, I'll check the bridge and see."

He left her standing at the water's edge. In the light she could see that he moved with care, slowly checking each board of the flooring. He was thorough and meticulous in his inspection. With a little wave he stepped from the bridge to the island. She could not see him clearly now, for the moon had gone behind a cloud.

She waited patiently. Occasionally her attention was drawn to the noises of the lake. A bullfrog by the far shore broke into full-throated song, followed by the answering call of its mate. A small fish jumped, causing the splashing water to sparkle as the moon broke again from the clouds.

"Jamie?" A hand softly touched her shoulder.

Not thinking, she turned her head to brush an absent kiss on the fingers that rested on her shoulder. "Mike, I didn't hear you come back."

"I know." He kept his voice low, reluctant to break

the hush. "If you'll do exactly as I tell you and step very carefully, we can go over to the island."

Holding her hand in his, moving with great and deliberate care, he guided her across the arched bridge. Once they had stepped onto the island, he released her.

"This is moss, not grass!" Jamie exclaimed as she bent to stroke the brilliant green at her feet.

"This is actually a very large stone. There's a bit of soil at the very center, but most of it's sheer granite. Over the years a thick coating of moss has thrived where grass never could."

"This is wonderful. Can we go into the gazebo?"

"No, I'm sorry. The floor has almost totally rotted away. But we can sit here on the moss for a while, if you'd like."

Jamie looked forlornly at the ancient structure, her disappointment showing clearly on her face. "It's really a shame this beautiful old thing is wasting away. I wish I could have seen it when it was in good condition."

"It was a special place, but that was long ago, Jamie," he said softly, then waited until she turned her face to his. "Come sit with me."

She moved to his side, and they both sat down on the moss with their backs to the gazebo. Before them was the lake, the moss-covered shore, and the softly rolling meadow.

"Mmm, this is like a velvet cushion. I think I could sit here all night." She stroked the smooth surface of the moss at her side.

"Do you have any idea how beautiful you are?"

The words were hardly more than a breath, they were so softly spoken.

"Don't, Mike."

"Why not? Can't I tell you how lovely you are?" A husky urgency throbbed in his voice.

"I'm not beautiful." Her hair swayed over her shoulders as she shook her head.

"You try not to be, but it doesn't work." His hands were in her hair. The damp air had turned each strand into a soft curl. "Your beauty's there despite your efforts to deny it. Even when you pull this glorious hair back into that tight knot, it's beautiful. That amazingly small body that you drape with austere little business suits is nonetheless exciting. In fact, my little Jamie, your pitiful efforts accomplish exactly the opposite of what you intend." He laughed at her hiss of indignation.

"What does that mean?"

"I mean, honey, that the tighter you twist your hair away, the more you make a man want to get his fingers into it. The first time I saw you, I could hardly keep from spilling it from its neat coil. I wanted to wind it around my hands and bind you to me. And don't be fooled into thinking those coldly sophisticated clothes mask the sexy grace of your body. I don't dare tell you what I wanted after only one good look at you. You're not ready to hear it. Not yet. But I will tell you this, Jamie. You're a fake, an impostor. Hiding behind that aloof, businesslike exterior is a warm, loving, and a very sensual woman . . . and she's mine."

Before she could refuse him, his lips took bold possession of hers. He slowly lowered her to the cush-

ioning moss, his body pressing her down. Sweetly, ur-
gently, he caressed the softness of her mouth, the easy
pressure ever deepening, touching only lightly. Yet all
the while he was capturing, holding, branding, and en-
ticing her further into enchantment.

In trancelike wonder her hands touched his chest
and slid up to frame his face. Seeking fingers found the
richness of his hair, and it was she who drew him
closer in breathtaking need. With the first touch of his
tongue against the satin curve of her lips, she surren-
dered to the ultimate consummation of a lover's kiss.
Eagerly he captured the secrets she offered. Lovingly
he taunted and teased, tantalizing, drawing her deeper
into unquenchable desire.

He drew back to gaze into the secret depths of her
eyes. His hand stroked her neck, then fastened around
the rabbit's foot that lay at her breast. Slowly, gently, he
drew the zipper down, parting the sweatshirt as if it
were the grandest of gowns.

"Naughty girl," he scolded when he saw the lacy
scallops of the sheer black bra. One finger traced the
edge of the lace as it molded the soft swell, pausing at
the clasp between her breasts. His head swooped
down and his mouth traced the path his finger had followed. He trailed tiny kisses at the cleft, then took her
budding nipple into his mouth. Through the sheer lace
she could feel the pleasing roughness of his tongue.

"As exquisite as it is, you don't need this." Deftly,
with a flick of his wrist, the clasp was released and the
lace parted. "Dear God, you're beautiful."

This time when his mouth sought her tender flesh,
she clasped him to her. Gone was the passive child;

Mike had awakened the woman. She reveled again in the pleasing rasp of the tongue that caressed the tips of her breasts. With his hands he shaped the contours of her body even as his lips continued to tantalize. Like a child he suckled, murmuring softly the endearments of love.

In a quick move he drew away, but only long enough to slip his own shirt over his head. He tossed it aside and leaned hungrily to kiss her again. As his bare skin warmed hers, Jamie was engulfed by the flames of desire. She touched him with urgent hands, her fingers stroking the rippling muscles of his back. Lightly her seeking palms brushed over his shoulders, his ribs, then his hips, which were tightly encased in denim.

"Jamie?" Mike murmured into her hair. "Do you know what you're doing?"

"No." She laughed huskily. "I'm quite sure that I don't. You and this place have bewitched me."

"I don't want you to make a mistake." Desperately he moved from her, his arms supporting his body as he looked down at her. Only the crisp, curling hair on his chest brushed her bare skin.

"Kiss me again, Mike." She reached to draw him back to her.

"I want you, Jamie Brent. I want you for my own, and if I kiss you now, there'll be no turning back. Listen to me, Jamie, and hear what I'm saying." His words were a plea to which she was deaf.

"Mike, please." Unconsciously she arched to brush her hardened nipples against him.

"God forgive me." Finally he answered her need. Reluctantly and just as helplessly, his lips met hers.

Gently his hands found her and soothed her aching
breasts. With great tenderness he caressed her and
kissed her, until at last his fingers closed over the snap
of her jeans. Releasing it, he hesitated for only a moment, then stroking her smooth skin, he traced a path
of fire over her midriff, his tongue teasing and tasting
her sweetness. The sheer lace of her panties proved no
deterrent.

"Naughty panties just for me," he whispered as his
tongue filled the slight depression of her navel. "Jamie,
Jamie. I need to love you. I need to love you now.
I—Herman!"

Mike sat up abruptly, leaving Jamie chilled and
confused. Tears of frustration gathered in her eyes, then
sanity slowly returned and she realized what she had
almost done.

"Herman," she heard Mike's voice through a haze
of painful embarrassment, "there's nothing I'd like
more this minute than to turn you into duck soup."

Jamie opened her tightly closed eyes to find herself face-to-face with the imperious duck she had fed at
dinner. She sat up, furtively fastening her bra and jeans,
then zipping her shirt firmly to her neck. Mike was slipping his own shirt over his head and she was spared,
for a precious moment, the shame of facing him.

Herman whimpered most pitifully, nudged Jamie's
shoulder, then whimpered again.

"Mike! Herman's hurt," she exclaimed, any thought
of herself forgotten in her concern for the wily bird.
"There's some sort of wire wrapped around him."

In an instant Mike was on his knees beside the injured duck. The wire was actually an old fishing line

and its hook had caught in his wing. Carefully cutting the line with his pocket knife, Mike was relieved to find that the hook had barely penetrated the skin. In a matter of minutes the duck was free and waddled ungratefully off to the lake.

Utterly still, with only the moonlight to show the even rise and fall of his breathing, Mike watched the duck as it swam away. Then, with a gentle and understanding smile on his face, he turned to Jamie.

"Come on, honey." He took her hand and pulled her to her feet. "I think it's past time I took you home."

Chapter Five

After a very silent walk back, Mike left Jamie at her door with only the lightest of kisses dropped casually on her forehead. "I'll call you, honey. Sleep well."

With that succinct farewell he was gone. Jamie moved about her apartment as if in a trance. The only sound was her occasional muttering as she stripped off her shirt and jeans. Stalking nude to the bathroom, she stuffed them into the laundry hamper, then pulled a frothy excuse for a nightgown over her head.

"Naughty, naughty," she mimicked as she grimaced into the mirror. "Tell me, Mr. Mike Bradford. Who wrote the law saying pretty lingerie was for the appreciation of a man only? Who says I can't wear it for myself alone?"

Indignantly she reached for her hairbrush. In only

two strokes she realized she was in for a long night of fighting tangles in the waist-length curls. In stubborn determination she tried to force the brush where it simply could not go. Gingerly she rubbed her aching scalp and admitted ruefully that patience was the only solution. Slowly she began to work the brush through her hair.

"Okay, Short Stuff," she leaned forward to glare at her image, "why do you bother? Why don't you get a haircut? Then you wouldn't have to fight this mess night after night. But then it would curl even more and tangle worse." She tossed the brush down in disgust, leaving the problem for tomorrow. Exasperated, she threw herself onto the bed, her chin propped on her folded hands.

"It's time to face facts, Jamie. Your hair is the least of your troubles. After tonight how will you ever face the man? Ha! After tonight, maybe you won't have to face him again." With a shuddering sigh she rolled over onto her back, her hands behind her head. "Who're you kidding? He'll be back. And what, you stupid fool, do you plan to do for an encore?

"Arrgh!" The exasperated cry curled her lips. "This must be your night for stupid questions. If you don't get some breathing space, the encore is a foregone conclusion—and if you don't stop talking to yourself, you're going to be locked up as a loony!"

In one graceful bound she left the bed and stripped off the naughty nightgown. She dug her jeans and shirt back out of the hamper and in seconds was redressed, down to the ragged tennis shoes. She sat down to dial a phone number.

"Hi, Meg, it's me. Hope I didn't interrupt anything." She paused, chuckling at a snappy rejoinder. "Tough. Maybe next time. You can always hope. Uh . . . could you take care of the office next week? I think I'd like to take part of my vacation early. You can? Great! Then I'll see you a week from Monday. Bye, Meg, and thanks."

The receiver dropped back into its cradle with a clatter, and Jamie stepped to her closet. She pulled out a battered duffle bag and began to stuff a variety of jeans, shirts, and dainty lingerie into it. Snapping it closed with a flourish, she stood utterly still. Her fingers flexed around the frayed grip of the bag as she looked once more at the telephone. Before she knew it, her hand was hovering uncertainly over it.

"No." She drew back sharply. "If I call him, if I let him know where I am, he won't let me have the space I need. Then I'd never be able to think this thing through. And anyway"—she spoke as if it were the real solution to her quandary—"I don't know his number."

In a quick turn she lifted the bag from the bed and swept from the room. Quietly she made her escape from the building. Luck was with her: the peanut gallery wasn't in the lobby. She had made a perfect getaway. Sighing with relief, she climbed into her car, thinking that a few days with her boisterous family was exactly what she needed to banish from her thoughts the beguiling Mike Bradford.

The drive across town took very little time. Actually Logansville was a small city when compared to nearby Atlanta. Traffic was light, and in a matter of minutes she had parked her car at the curb in front of her parents' rambling old house.

"Mom? Dad?" she called as she let herself in with her key. There was no answer. Shrugging, she decided it was just as well no one was home. Tomorrow would be soon enough to face the inevitable questions about Suzy Sanderson's column.

Taking the stairs two at a time, she made her way to her old room. In seconds she was again dressed in the nightgown and without ceremony she crawled into the bed that was always ready and waiting for her return. As she drifted into sleep she murmured, "Tomorrow, Jamie, you have to begin to decide what to do about Mike Bradford."

"Good morning. Sleep well?" Carol Brent greeted her daughter as if she were there for breakfast every morning.

"Sure did. Mmm, something smells good."

"It's your favorite coffee cake. Sit down, it's almost ready."

"Where's Dad?" Jamie sat sipping from the cup her mother had set before her.

"He left early. The golf finals are today."

Jamie watched as her mother moved efficiently about her chores. "How did you do it, Mom?"

"How did I do what?"

"How did you take care of this house and this wild crew and still have time for the special things you've always done for us? Even when you were playing tennis, we always got more than our share of your attention."

"It wasn't hard, Jamie. I loved you."

"It must have been awfully difficult at times."

"Not really, but there were times I felt guilty about you. I'm afraid that as the only girl in the crowd you got lost in the shuffle."

"No, I didn't. Sure, having six brothers who were such terrific athletes helped to influence the direction of my life. They were good. I wanted to be just as good. For you, for them, and for myself."

"And now?" Carol watched every expression that crossed Jamie's face. "It's been years since you were able to compete. Now you've left teaching. Didn't it fill the void?"

"For a while it did." She grinned at her mother. "Until I got homesick."

"Will you go back?"

"To teaching maybe. But not to France. I love Georgia. It's where I'd like to stay. Working as a translator for the Bradford Corporation may not be a challenge, but it's different from anything I've ever done. It keeps me busy, and for now that's enough."

"Is it truly enough? There's another side to life that you're neglecting."

"Men, you mean." Jamie stared down into her cup. "My life's not totally devoid of them, you know. There've been several."

"Yes, there have been," Carol agreed. "And with each it's been the same. You battled them at tennis and racquetball, outswam them, outhiked them, and treated each one as if he were one of your brothers. Those who would settle for that have become good friends; those who wanted more have moved on. You're a beautiful woman, Jamie. You're also a mature, vibrant person. Men find you attractive and desirable. It's something you're going to have to come to terms with. Someday you're going to meet a man who will neither accept the role of surrogate brother, nor go away. What will you do then?"

Before Jamie could answer, heavy footsteps sounded across the porch and two tall men entered the kitchen, golf bags over their shoulders. The older man saw Jamie first, his face brightening into a beaming smile.

"Jamie girl, how are you this morning?"

"Terrific, Dad." She raised her face for his kiss, thankful for the interruption. "Have you finished your golf match already?"

"No, I forgot a new club I wanted to try."

"Since you're here, I'll bet you'd like to come along and caddy for me," her brother Andrew teased.

"Wouldn't I just!"

Her father broke into the familiar routine. "How long will you be with us, Jamie?"

"A week."

"Good." He nodded. "Early vacation?"

"Yep."

"I hope you brought your work clothes. I need some help in the yard."

"I brought my grubbiest stuff and I'm at your service." Jamie smiled at him. "We haven't done that in a long time."

"Not since you pulled up my petunias for weeds."

"Then you banned me from your garden for the rest of the summer."

"I always suspected you did it to escape garden

duty." The twinkle in her father's eyes told her he had been wise to her ploy from the first.

"I'll never tell," Jamie declared, "but I can promise you, I know the difference now."

"I'd better get that club so we can be going, Andrew." With a smile and a kiss for Carol, Larry Brent left the room with Andrew close behind.

"Hey, kid." Andrew stuck his head around the doorway. "You wouldn't want to reconsider and come be my caddy, would you?"

"No thanks, I'll pass up that illustrious opportunity."

"I guess it's for the best. You're such a runt, I'd mistake you for a club and stuff you in the bag too." He ducked behind the closing door as Jamie's napkin bounced off the spot where his head had been.

"Brothers! The scourge of the earth, and I have six!"

"You love them—every one," Carol added, chuckling.

"Yeah, I guess I do." Jamie stood, gathering up her dishes. "Do you want these in the dishwasher?"

"There's not enough to bother. I'll wash, you dry."

They talked quietly as they worked. Jamie waited for her mother to mention the newspaper column, but she didn't. "Uh, Mom?"

Carol finished the last of the dishes and turned to face her daughter. "Let's sit on the porch and you can tell me what's bothering you."

For a long while they sat side by side in the comfortable rocking chairs that were almost as old as Jamie. At last Carol prompted gently, "Jamie?"

"Oh, Mom, don't pretend you haven't seen it."

"Suzy Sanderson's column, you mean?"

"Yes, it's awful, isn't it?"

"That depends."

"On what, for heaven's sake?"

"Whether or not it's true," her mother answered.

"That's the problem. Some of it's true, some isn't."

"That's about what I suspected. Would you like to tell me about it?"

"It's crazy. I knocked a man down before the can could, and skinned my knee. . . . He carried me down the street and told the doctor I was an injured midget. . . . Then I got six dozen pairs of pantyhose by special delivery. . . . Lisa Lang asked if she could have him. . . . Then the reporters came and Mike got mad when one asked if we were lovers. . . . Jean-Charles brought dinner to my apartment. . . . Mike knew all my favorite things. . . . I told him about David. . . . He says he can't tell the reporters I'm not his fiancée or they'll think I'm his mistress. . . . I dressed in my old jeans and ragged shirt, but his were worse. . . . He asked the peanut gallery to watch out for me. . . ."

Jamie paused for breath and left her chair to pace the porch. Her mother wisely did not speak, but waited for the torrent to begin again. Jamie stopped her pacing and whirled to face Carol.

"Even as awful as I looked, we went to a secret little park. . . . Cholie made me hot dogs and sodas. . . . We fed the ducks. . . . On a nature trail we saw deer drinking from a lake and we crossed a rickety bridge to the island—except it's not an island, it's a rock. . . . The poor gazebo is too rotted and I couldn't go inside, so

we sat on the moss and Mike kissed me. . . . Poor
Herman got caught in a fishing line and saved me. . . .
Mike cut him loose and when he was gone we came
back to my apartment." She stopped abruptly, her eyes
pleading for understanding. "So you see, I had to come
here. I had to get away. Can you understand?"

"Well, if I give it enough time, I think I will. You
only left out two things. You've already met the man
who refuses to become a brother and I don't think he's
going away. You love him, don't you, Jamie?"

"I don't! I can't! I've only known him two days."

"How long does it take, sweetheart?"

"Whatever it is, it hasn't taken him very long.
Mom, he hasn't kissed me—I mean, really kissed me—
more than twice. Both times I've been ready to lay my
world at his feet. In fact, if it hadn't been for
Herman . . ." Jamie let her voice trail away, leaving the
rest for her mother to surmise.

"You must introduce me to Herman one day. He
sounds like a very interesting man. Got caught in his
own fishing line, did you say?"

"Oh, Mom." Jamie giggled. "Herman's not a man,
he's a duck."

"Oh, a duck." Carol nodded. "You did say you fed
the ducks. This duck rescued you?"

"Yes, from making a fool of myself because of this
. . . this . . . sexual attraction. Yes! That's what it is!
Simply a case of sexual attraction. But," Jamie added
hastily, "you wouldn't understand that."

"I wouldn't? Have you forgotten I have seven children?"

"With you and Dad it's different."

"Jamie, there's love and there's sexual attraction. They don't necessarily go together, but when they do, it's beautiful. Your dad and I have that rare combination. Perhaps you will too. Remember, love can come suddenly. It's the nurturing that makes it last and grow. If you have that rare and precious thing, handle it with care."

"Then you aren't shocked?"

"After six sons, a beautiful daughter, and thirty-five years with your father, nothing surprises me anymore."

"Has the rest of the family seen the article?"

"I'm afraid your Aunt Prue saw to it that they did, but maybe she'll forget about it after a while."

"Fat chance! There's more. Mike promised Suzy the inside story of our—uh, romance if she wouldn't publish any more innuendos. He plans to give her bits of information, to keep her happy."

"That sounds like a sensible thing to do. Mike must be a very wise man. You could do worse. Perhaps this was all meant to be."

"Don't start that! You sound like him, and one Mike Bradford is more than enough."

"Why don't I show you your father's rock garden and we won't think about this situation anymore?"

They walked in the bright sunlight, both heads shining like a raven's wing. Jamie slanted a glance at her mother as they neared the garden. Carol was amazingly youthful for a woman who had borne her first child at eighteen, then another each year or two with maddening regularity. When she was twenty-six, Jamie had been born prematurely exactly ten months after the twins, Scott and Steve. For a while her mother's health had been poor and the money short, but never the love.

"Carol? Carol? Where are you?"

The strident voice shattered the peace of the moment. Stalking across the lawn with the fire of the self-righteous flaming in her eyes was Aunt Prue—the self-appointed conscience of the family.

"Have you read this awful article in the morning paper?"

"Yes, Prue." Carol sighed resignedly. "But I'm sure you'll enlighten me anyway."

"Jamie! Well, I certainly didn't expect to see *you* here!" Prue drew her spare, angular body even more erect. There were the remnants of beauty still visible in her haughty face. Beauty that had been destroyed by the constant expressions of unrelenting pride and disapproval. Her accusing eyes fastened on Jamie.

"Why should you be surprised to see Jamie here, Prue? After all, this has always been her home and it always will be," Carol interjected mildly, forestalling Jamie's answer.

"I should think she wouldn't want to face her family just now."

"And why not?" The soft control of her mother's voice signaled to Jamie how angry she had become. Over the years they had all learned that the angrier Carol became, the softer her voice grew. Prue, too, after all this time as Carol's sister-in-law, should have known and heeded. Instead, in her usual insensitive manner, she stabbed for the heart.

"You read that disgraceful article yesterday. I

showed it to both you and Larry. It all but called Jamie a . . . a . . ."

"If you're wise, Prue, you'll stop right there. You've said more than enough on the subject. You've destroyed your own life with your prudery, but not Jamie's. You'll say no more about the matter." There was quiet steel in the gentle voice. "I suggest that you remember such columns often hint at what they don't know. Hell! I can't understand why an intelligent person would make a practice of reading such trash."

Prue sniffed disdainfully. "I don't suppose I should be surprised at that attitude, coming from you. Not after the way you've acted with my brother. It's in the blood. Like mother, like daughter."

"I certainly hope so!" Carol rose to her feet, facing Prue with glazing eyes. "I hope Jamie will someday have what I have. I may not be a saint, but I'd rather she be like me than like you. Our home is filled with the love and laughter of mortal people. People who are far from perfect. People who can reach out and give of themselves. What has your pristine perfection gotten you? Are you happy? Is that empty bed of yours reward enough for the unbending code you live by?"

"How dare you?" Prue sputtered and would have said more, but the irate Carol was not through.

"I dare that and a great deal more when one of my children is maligned. How dare *you* come here and presume to judge? I don't for one minute think Jamie's guilty of any terrible sin, but even if she were, at twenty-six I'd say it's her business."

"Of all the—"

"Just a minute, I'm not through. As for the paper,

I've read it. It's not my usual choice of good entertainment, but yes, this morning I read it! Jamie knows that Suzy will be printing more about her romance with Mike." Carol's lips twitched with a mischievous smile at Prue's shocked face. "Yes, Prue, there is a romance. That part was the gospel truth. Now, perhaps you'll tell me where the evil lies in two young people being seen strolling through a park holding hands. For normal young lovers it's a natural course of action. But you wouldn't understand about that. More's the pity."

"Young lovers, indeed," Prue huffed. "You seem to forget that the rest of the article said they disappeared into the woods. What nice girl would be seen going into the woods with a man?"

"May the good Lord deliver me from such stupidity! Prue, it was a beautiful morning before you arrived, maybe it can be again. Leave! Go peddle your own personal brand of evil somewhere else." Again Carol's voice dropped into the ominously low cadence. "There's just one more thing. Don't be spreading your vitriolic opinions about. Feel free to think what you will, but if you're wise, your opinion will remain strictly your own. There are those who won't take kindly to hearing you repeat the vicious things you've just said."

"Who has the right to say what I can talk about, and to whom?"

"Larry for one, and I strongly suspect Mike Bradford for another. Then, of course, there are Jamie's brothers. You haven't forgotten about them, have you?"

"Are you threatening me?" The voice was still strident, but there was the first faltering of confidence as it broke slightly.

"Not threatening, only warning."

"Larry's going to hear about how you've spoken to me today!"

"Be my guest." Carol smiled, her anger scattered by the hilarious notion of prim, proper Prue tattling to the man who thought Carol could do no wrong.

The poorly disguised laughter of mother and daughter was the last straw. Prue turned on her heel to stalk again across the lawn like an avenging angel. Around the house and onto the drive she marched, pausing impatiently for the car that had turned into it. Even from a distance Carol and Jamie could hear her shrill voice as she berated a bewildered Simon, Jamie's older brother, for blocking her way.

"I've never seen anything like that before." Jamie looked at her mother in awe. "I've never heard anyone speak to her so bluntly, and I've never seen you so angry."

"A long time ago I decided that Prue was more to be pitied than taken seriously, but that was before she turned her hate on one of my children. Maybe it's past time someone put an end to her maliciousness. I've tried to excuse her behavior as that of a lonely, bitter woman."

Carol grasped both Jamie's hands and pulled her to her feet. "Unless I miss my guess, we're about to be invaded again, this time by friendly forces."

"Gramma, Gramma!" An impatient young voice sounded across the yard. "Where are you, Gramma?"

"Here, Sam, down by the creek," Carol called, and in seconds a small, compact body propelled by short, sturdy legs catapulted into her arms.

"Gramma, we come to see you," the golden-haired cherub proclaimed with great relish. "We hope you maked us some chocolate cookies, an . . . an . . . Uncle Jamie!" The child interrupted himself with a squeal of delight as Jamie's presence penetrated his total absorption with his grandmother. "We didn't know you were here." Happily the child stretched his arms to Jamie.

"Hello, Sam." She laughed as she accepted the wriggling bundle from her mother. "How are *we* today?"

"We fine. Have you had any chocolate cookies, Uncle Jamie?"

"No, Sam." She smiled down into the delightfully innocent face of Simon's child. "But I'll bet we could find some if we sneak into the pantry. C'mon, let's go see." She rested the child on a rock and turned so that he could climb on to ride piggyback.

"Giddap!" Sam clutched her shoulder, shouting and giggling madly as she galloped across the stepping stones. Carol followed at a more sedate pace, an indulgent smile on her face.

"Daddy! Daddy! Uncle Jamie's here."

"So I see." The tall dark-haired man smiled at his sister. Bending to kiss her, he murmured, "How are you, *Uncle* Jamie? How's the horse?"

"Hi, Simon. The horse is fine, but the jockey needs a cookie. We're off to raid the pantry. See you later." The last words drifted over her shoulder as she jogged up the steps and into the house.

Simon watched them disappear into the kitchen then turned to kiss his mother's cheek. "Are you all right, Mom? Aunt Prue was in rare form today. What ticked her off?"

"Suzy Sanderson."

"Oh, that. What did Jamie say?"

"Nothing. I'm afraid I said it all."

"You lost your temper?"

"I did!"

"Terrific! It's time someone shut up that busy-body." Simon linked his arm through hers. "Let's go see if Sam and Uncle Jamie found your cookies. Simon likes them too."

Laughter, deep and light, floated across the peaceful lawn as mother and son followed to join in the cookie raid.

"Drat!"

"Something wrong, Jamie girl?" Her father looked at her over the top of the evening paper.

"I forgot my needlework. I'll need to stitch some every day if I'm to have it finished by Sunday."

"Something special?"

Jamie nodded as she searched in her purse for her car keys. "A cross-stitch of the Duke Blue Devil. I've decided that for each of my brother's birthdays I'm going to cross-stitch their college mascots."

"A wolf, a ram, a bulldog, two tigers, and a blue devil. Except for the last, it sounds like a zoo." Carol laughed at her own joke.

"Does, doesn't it? Ah-ha! Found them!" Jamie triumphantly drew out her keys. "I'm going to run over to my apartment."

"Would you like me to ride over with you?"

"No need, Dad. I can be there and back before you finish the paper."

"You're sure you'll be all right?"

"Positive." Jamie hid her grin. Even though she had spent years living alone and in a foreign country, her father still worried when she drove across town by herself. "I'll be back before you know it."

The trip took longer than expected. She decided to water a drooping violet and the straggly ferns she had been lavishing with tender care. "Jamie," she muttered as she broke off a brown stalk, "you definitely have a brown thumb."

The telephone at her side rang, cutting through the silence. Thinking it would be her father at his protective best, she answered cheerfully, "Brent's Mortuary. You stab 'em, we slab 'em."

Without a second's hesitation the reply came. "If you have one who's not quite cold and answers to the name of Jamie, I'd like to speak to her, if I might."

Jamie held the receiver in a tight grip. It felt as if it were glued to her ear. No words would come.

"Jamie, honey, are you there?"

"Mike?"

"None other." He chuckled. "Were you expecting someone else?"

"I thought you were my dad," she blurted.

"Hardly."

"Sorry about the silly greeting. It's a joke left over from childhood."

"I missed you this morning. Monday morning is bad enough, but without you it's worse." His voice was low and seductively resonant, and he ignored her explanation as if he had not heard it.

"I—I had some errands to run. I was late this morning." It was an impetuous lie, but if he knew it he made no comment.

"Did you sleep well last night, Jamie? I couldn't. I haven't since Friday. I keep seeing you as you looked in the moonlight with your hair like black silver streaming over your shoulders. Diamonds and furs couldn't have been as lovely as that sweatshirt and jeans. You don't really need to wear a bra, but I'm glad you do. That wicked creation you wore was enchanting."

"Mike."

"All I have to do is close my eyes and it all comes back. I can see every curve and how the lace clung, teasing me with your hidden beauty."

"Mike!"

"You're here with me, Jamie. In my thoughts and my dreams until I ache for you."

"Don't," she protested weakly.

"Haven't you thought of me? Can you put me from your mind? Aren't I with you every moment, as you are with me?"

"No." The single word was a half whisper of little conviction.

"Sweet little liar." He chuckled.

"Mike, I have to go."

"Running, honey?"

"Of course not." She tried to cover her confusion with indignation. "Why should I run? I'm not afraid of you."

"No," he agreed softly, "only of yourself. You're a

passionate woman, Jamie Brent, but you've locked it
away, trying to deny it. I intend to wipe away your
fears. You can't trust me, darling, until you trust yourself, and what we share must be based on trust. I won't
settle for anything less."

"Why bother? Why don't you find someone who
suits you better than I? Surely there are other women
who would be more than happy to be whatever you
want them to be."

"No other woman would be Jamie Brent. I
wouldn't belong to them as I do to you. Have you forgotten that I'm yours and have been since the day you
saved my life?"

"I really do have to go now, Mike." Jamie knew
that if she listened to his soft, soothing voice any
longer, she would be caught in the magic he was weaving. How could only the sound of his voice do this to
her? What hope could she have of resisting him? Now
she was truly frightened, and it was indeed of herself.

"Run if you feel you must. Soon you'll be running
to me, Jamie. I'll wait for that day, and I'll be as patient
as I can."

Very gently Jamie replaced the receive and fled
once more to the sanctuary of her parents' home.

Once she had put Mike's call determinedly from her
mind, Jamie spent a lazy and relaxing week. It was
hard to believe that this old-fashioned house with its
rolling lawns and aged giant oaks was situated on the
outskirts of a small but growing city. On a long,
shaded, winding street that was laid out when the city
was only a village, and *suburb* nothing more than a

Passion awaits you...
Step into the magical world of

Loveswept

E N J O Y . . .

6 ROMANCES RISK FREE!

PLUS **FREE GIFT**

Detach and affix this stamp to the reply card and mail at once!

Enjoy Kay Hooper's *"Larger Than Life"*! Not for sale anywhere, this exclusive novel is yours to keep—FREE— no matter what!

S E E   D E T A I L S   I N S I D E . . .

A Magical World of Enchantment Awaits You When You're Loveswept!

Your heart will be swept away with Loveswept Romances when you meet exciting heroes you'll fall in love with...beautiful heroines you'll identify with. Share the laughter, tears and the passion of unforgettable couples as love works its magic spell. These romances will lift you into the exciting world of love, charm and enchantment!

You'll enjoy award-winning authors such as Iris Johansen, Sandra Brown, Kay Hooper and others who top the best-seller lists. Each offers a kaleidoscope of adventure and passion that will enthrall, excite and exhilarate you with the magic of being Loveswept!

- ♥ *We'd like to send you 6 new novels to enjoy—risk free!*
- ♥ *There's no obligation to buy.*
- ♥ *6 exciting romances—plus your free gift—brought right to your door!*
- ♥ *Convenient money-saving, time-saving home delivery!*

Join the Loveswept at-home reader service and we'll send you 6 new romances about once a month— before they appear in the bookstore! You always get 15 days to preview them before you decide. Keep only those you want. Each book is yours for only $2.25* That's a total savings of $3.00 off the retail price for each 6 book shipment.

*plus shipping & handling and sales tax in NY and Canada

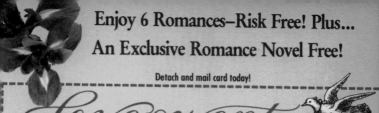

Enjoy 6 Romances–Risk Free! Plus...
An Exclusive Romance Novel Free!

Detach and mail card today!

Loveswept

AFFIX RISK FREE BOOK STAMP HERE.

Yes! Please send my 6 Love-swept novels RISK FREE along with the exclusive romance novel "Larger Than Life" as my <u>free gift</u> to keep.

RE123 412 28

....
N A M E

....
A D D R E S S   A P T .

....
C I T Y

....
S T A T E   Z I P

MY ''NO RISK''
Guarantee

I understand when I accept your offer for Loveswept Romances I'll receive the 6 newest Loveswept novels right at home about once a month (before they're in bookstores!). I'll have 15 days to look them over. If I don't like the books, I'll simply return them and owe nothing. You even pay the return postage. Otherwise, I'll pay just $2.25 per book (plus shipping & handling & sales tax in NY and Canada). I *save* $3.00 off the retail price of the 6 books! I understand there's no obligation to buy and I can cancel anytime. No matter what, the gift is mine to keep–*free!*

SEND NO MONEY NOW.
Prices subject to change. Orders subject to approval. Prices shown are U.S. prices.

ENJOY...

FREE BOOK OFFER
RUSH!

BUSINESS REPLY MAIL

FIRST CLASS MAIL   PERMIT NO. 2456   HICKSVILLE, NY

POSTAGE WILL BE PAID BY ADDRESSEE

LOVESWEPT
BANTAM DOUBLEDAY DELL DIRECT
PO BOX 985
HICKSVILLE NY 11802-9827

NO POSTAGE
NECESSARY
IF MAILED
IN THE
UNITED STATES

word applied to the future, theirs was a peaceful neighborhood, only miles from the hub of the city, yet light-years away in thought and deed. Lawn mowers and laughter filled the days as friends and neighbors called greetings while they clipped, snipped, and pruned their already well-groomed lawns.

A hodgepodge of young and old, the neighborhood thrived on the harmony of a close-knit community. It was not uncommon to see families gathered over a barbecue grill or an ice cream churn as twilight fell over the sleepy Georgia countryside.

Curiously Jamie was acutely aware of these things for the first time and found them inordinately pleasing. She could hardly believe she had once been eager to get away and forget this part of her life as well as her shattered dreams. In the months since her return from France she had become a frequent, welcome visitor, happily absorbing the genuine pleasures of a loving, tranquil home.

For the first time in years she took part in family life with a zest that was real, not pretended. She welcomed the impromptu visits and the unplanned dinners that only a large, unruly family could orchestrate. Each day she grew more tan and more curvaceous, thanks to the work in her father's gardens and her mother's cooking. Thoughts of her life on the other side of the city seldom crossed her mine. It was another time, another life, another planet.

Only one thought, disturbing and unsettling, crept past her firm resolve, reminding her that no matter how idyllic these days were, tomorrow would come—and with the problems of yesterday. Without warning

Mike's image would materialize, boldly and irrevocably. Then she would invariably lose the thread of conversation or forget her tasks. She wasn't aware of how often her family exchanged knowing looks over her preoccupied head. Nor did she realize how transparent she was when she dragged her attention back to the matter at hand, firmly forbidding herself to think of Mike. At these times she became the instigator of pranks and the organizer of games in a frenzied attempt to blot the intruder from her mind. Sometimes the ploy was successful, but gradually and insidiously it became less so. With understanding patience her brothers watched as, often in the middle of an escapade, she would wander away, lost in her private thoughts, to a place separate from the group. And for the first time ever they did not tease.

Only one small article appeared in the Suzy Sanderson column that week, hinting that since there was no news, there was a serious romance afoot. She wrote:

> The elusive reclusive continues to protect his lady with a cloak of silence. In the past when pursued, this divine man has let the adventuress sink or swim in her own publicity. How many foolish hopefuls have enlisted the aid of the press, only to go down in defeat? Not so this dark-haired beauty. Is it love or the wisdom of a wily enchantress?

And Jamie waited. She waited for the questions and the teasing that never came.

Chapter Six

Sunday dawned clear and beautiful, and with it the last day of Jamie's sanctuary. After church the entire family gathered at the Brent home. Simon and his wife, Carla, were there with their two sons. Nicky, at nine, was the oldest, and the irrepressible Sam was three. Alex, who at thirty-two was two years younger than Simon, was alone. His fiancée, a stewardess, was based in Kansas for the weekend. Seth and his very pregnant wife, Jenny, came late, followed by twenty-nine-year-old Andrew. Scott and Steve, the twins who were less than a year older than Jamie, had spent the weekend with their parents.

The day was a festive one, for not only did they enjoy being together, they were celebrating Seth's thirtieth birthday. Teasing was the order of the day, but still never directed at the wary Jamie.

At last, unable to bear the suspense for a moment longer, it was she who broached the subject. "Seth, have you seen the articles in the paper?"

"You mean the Sanderson columns?"

"Of course."

"Sure, I saw them. With Aunt Prue on the prowl how could anyone miss them?"

"Well?" Jamie was emphatically impatient.

"Well, what?"

"What did you think of them?"

"What am I supposed to think?"

"For crying out loud! Did it upset you that she hinted—uh, that I was—oh, Seth, you know what I mean."

"Jamie, you're twenty-six years old. Old enough to lead your own life. Why should it matter what I think?" The tall, muscular young man dropped an arm about her shoulder. "But if it makes you feel any better, it didn't bother me at all. In fact, I'd say it's past time you had a fuller life. To be honest I would like to meet this man. We all want to look him over to see if he's good enough for our kid sister, but none of us has any intention of passing judgment. Anyway"—he moved his arm from her and swatted her playfully on the backside— "Jenny's more than I can handle at the moment. I get nervous just looking at her. Do you realize today could be the day?"

"Yeah, little brother." Simon joined them. "Since you're about to join the ranks of fatherhood, you do have your hands full. Alex is taking bets on who will be the most nervous, you or Dad. Mom's money's on Dad, but mine's on you to win hands down."

"Why is Dad so nervous?" Jamie asked. "It's not as if it's his first grandchild."

"Because he has his heart set on a little girl. He's impatient and afraid all at the same time. Yesterday he assured Jenny he'd love a little boy, but it surely would be nice to have a little girl in the family again." Seth chuckled as he watched his father playing tag with Nicky and Sam.

"He never really had a little girl in me, did he?" Jamie moved restlessly away from the tree she had leaned against. "From the very first I was a tomboy, having to compete with all of you." She, too, watched fondly as the chase centered around a prize rosebush. "I never realized until now how much we missed."

"What is it you missed, Jamie?" Simon spoke, but both brothers waited for her answer, concerned frowns marking the handsome faces.

"Oh, things like sharing that first date with him. The nervous teenager–protective father bit. Showing off my first prom dress to the first man in my life. Rushing home from college to show them both a fraternity pin or an engagement ring. Silly things to you, I suppose, but the stuff a young girl's dreams should be made of."

"You never had any of that, did you?" Seth stroked a stray curl from her shoulder.

"No." Bitterness welled within her. "When all the girls that age should be sharing with their families, I was down at the gym practicing."

"It was your choice," Simon reminded her, not unkindly.

"I know it was, and for the first time I can see that I wasn't the only one who suffered for it."

"And what about now?" Seth asked quietly. "You turned your back on a lifelong dream without a backward look. Have you been happy, Jamie? Are you doing what you want to with your life?"

"I don't know. Who really gets what she wants anyway?" she shrugged.

"It never hurts to try." Seth spoke so softly, Jamie hardly heard. "Look at Jenny, if you want proof. Did you know that two years ago she was told she would never carry a baby to term? And look at her now."

Jamie exchanged a look with Simon, each understanding the pride and love Seth felt for his young determined wife.

"This baby may be a miracle, but the biggest miracle is how you ever caught such a terrific gal," Simon teased. "The poor little thing must have had a temporary mental lapse. Let's face it, when Carla got me, she got the cream of the crop. The only one in the family anyone would want."

The verbal battle began. Seth and Simon were soon deep into a debate. Jamie listened for a few minutes, amazed at the agile mental footwork executed by both men. Then as so often happened, her interest flagged. Deep in thoughts of her own, she drifted away from the boisterous family and made her way across the lawn.

There was a huge oak down by the creek, and in its spreading branches was tucked an old battered treehouse. In truth it was little more than a few boards nailed across two limbs that dipped low over the bubbling water. Jamie had always come here to think and snatch at the dreams she was missing. She scrambled up the makeshift ladder nailed to the trunk, stretched full-length on the roughened boards, then with her hands behind her head watched the constantly changing clouds through the swaying leaves.

As ever, even in the midst of her family, she found solitude here; the creek at the base of the old tree sang to her as it swirled over its rocky bed. The gentle rustle of the leaves, the drone of the bees swooping to the water's edge, and laughter that floated in the air, lulled her into a restful sleep. The sun that slanted through the trees bathed her in a golden haze as the same breeze that played among the leaves lifted and teased tiny tendrils of her loose hair.

"Jamie?" Her mother's voice barely penetrated her sleepy lethargy.

"Mmm?" Jamie's muffled answer could not have been heard at the creek bank, and certainly not across the yard.

"Jamie?" The screen door slammed, echoing through the trees. "She must be down at the creek. I'll get her."

There was an indistinct murmur that Jamie, already drifting back into sleep, did not hear. A muted hush again settled over the day. Nothing moved but a brightly colored butterfly fluttering aimlessly in the sunlight.

Slow, measured treads and the whispering protest of the disturbed underbrush roused her only slightly. The scuff of a shoe against the ladder signaled that someone had come to join her. With her eyes still closed, she murmured, "Mom? Is that you?"

There was no answer as the shifting sounds

stopped and a gentle finger brushed over her eyelids. "Have you finished the dishes or have you come for re-inforcements?"

The hand that moved over her face lingered at her lips and a low chuckle caressed her ears. "The dishes are done, love, no thanks to you."

"Mike!" Jamie's eyes flew open and she found herself staring up into laughing eyes. "What're you doing here?"

"The last time I looked, I was sitting in a tree with you." His green gaze swept over her, lingering on the deep V of her bright blue halter, then moving over her snug white shorts to her tanned legs and bare toes.

"I mean, what are you doing here—here at my parents' house?" Blushing, she surreptitiously tugged at the bottom of her halter to draw it back over the undercurve of her breast. Silently she cursed the loose elastic that had slipped when she put her arms over her head.

"I would think my reason for being here was obvious. I came to see you."

"Why?"

"Because this has been a long week and I needed to see you and do this . . ." He leaned his head down to her, his lips gently closing her eyes.

"And this . . ." His lips touched the tip of her nose lightly.

"This . . ." He nibbled the line of her jaw, touching the slight cleft in her chin with his tongue.

"Then this . . ." Her earlobe was drawn into the warmth of his mouth and a shiver shook her shoulders.

The deep sound that rumbled in his chest was the purr of a pleased jungle cat.

"But most of all, I needed this. . . ." His mouth brushed hers fleetingly, lifted, then returned as though drawn like a moth to a flame. "Oh, yes; most of all—this."

His touch was no longer fleeting, but demanding; forbidding the passivity with which she had accepted his sensual explorations. This kiss, a loving assault, commanded that she join him in furor. To take and be given, to give and be taken. It was a silent demand that she match flame with fire, rapture with ecstasy, passion with ardor, to devastate and be devastated. It allowed no holding back, no hidden recesses, and Jamie met the challenge.

Her arms, resting at her side, slid of their own volition over the swell of his corded arms. Questing fingers played across his open collar to the hollow of his throat, then down to the buttons of his shirt. One by one, she slipped them free. She could feel the sudden halt of his breathing as she burrowed her fingers into the soft down on his chest. Slowly she traced the shape of his body, lingering at the small hard nipple that hid among the curled brown hair.

"Honey," he murmured against her lips, his breath sweet against her cheek, "I've missed you. This has been the longest week of my life."

"How did you know where to find me?" Jamie's hand explored the strong column of his neck, stopping to rest again at the hollow where his heart was pounding a wild staccato.

"No problem, I knew where you'd be," he growled between soft kisses.

"Meg told you," she said, her fingers at the pulse point beneath his ear.

"Nope. She's innocent this time. I've known where you were from the first." With his lips he smoothed a ruffled eyebrow.

"How could you know?" Inquisitively she traced the contours of his ear.

"Simple. I called your mother." His rich, vibrant voice had become less and less steady.

"You asked my mother?" Jamie was very still, her eyes open and watching him incredulously.

"Sure, why not?" He nudged his cheek against her hand, entreating that she continue her sweet, tantalizing forays.

"And just what else did you say to her?" she demanded, pinching his earlobe firmly between thumb and finger.

"I simply introduced myself"—a feathery kiss to her eyes—"asked if you were here and all right"—a quick brush over her cheek—"and asked her to call me if there were any problems."

"She never said a word!" Jamie exclaimed.

"I asked her not to."

"Why?"

"I didn't want to spoil your vacation."

"But you're here now."

"Yes, I am, aren't I?" A wicked grin flashed across his face. "So what're we going to do about it?"

"Well," she drawled as she slid her hands down his neck and throat to his chest, "how about this?" Quickly she gave a hard tug to the matted curls that peeked through his open shirt.

"Ouch! Witch!" In retaliation he nipped her lower lip, catching it between his even teeth. Gently, as he held it captive, he soothed it with the tip of his tongue. Releasing her, he drew back to look carefully into her eyes. "You know what you're doing this time, don't you?"

"Yes."

"Are you afraid?"

"Yes."

"Why, Jamie?"

"It's too fast. It's too much, too soon. I don't understand where it all came from or where it's going. All I know is that when you're near me, when you touch me, I can't think. What's wrong with me? Am I crazy?"

"No, honey. You're not crazy, or if you are, then I'm just as crazy. One look at you sitting in the dust of that deserted street, and I was lost. It was no joke when I said I was yours from that moment. It's true, just as surely as it's true that I'm going to kiss you again. Now."

"No! Wait." She tried to evade his insistent lips. "This is absolutely ridicu—"

The remainder of her objections was swallowed by the complete possession of his kiss. Again he demanded no less than all of her, and again, in spite of her protests, she conceded.

A bird called in the heat of the day. A butterfly rested for an instant on a leaf by Jamie's head, but neither she nor he was aware of anything but the trembling passion that was raging between them.

"Stop!" Jamie wrenched her mouth from his, a pleading hand rested at the side of his neck. "Please, we need to talk. Don't do this to me."

"All right, Jamie, if you insist." He slipped farther down on the hard surface of the weathered wood. Making himself as comfortable as possible, with his long legs dangling over the edge he stretched out beside her. His head rested at her shoulder with his cheek against the softness of her breast. "You talk, I'll listen."

Silence seemed to stretch interminably between them. Mike's hand stroked the silken hair he had spread over his arm. Sounds from the outside world drifted about them, but did not disrupt their haven. He waited patiently, then after long moments prompted gently.

"Jamie, you said you wanted to talk."

"I know." She laughed ruefully. "But suddenly I can't think of what to say."

"Say what you feel."

"That's the problem, Mike. I don't know what I feel."

"Yes, you do. You just refuse to admit it. But I'll give you time, however much you need."

"Don't patronize me!" She slapped his hand away from her hair.

"Jamie, I'm not patronizing you. I respect your intelligence and your proud spirit far too much to make that mistake. I was truthfully promising not to crowd you. Admittedly this won't be easy on me, but it is a promise. I won't pressure you or hurry you."

"There you go again," Jamie wailed. "Just when I have my defenses up, you say something sweet and understanding and I'm right back where I started. I'm beginning to think that I don't have any defenses against you."

"I hope not." His hand again stroked the lock of hair she had slapped away. It lay curled about her breast. With false innocence he smoothed it down her shoulder and over the tip to where it touched the bare skin of her midriff. He ignored the catch in her breath as he brushed the tautening crest. He pretended, as well, to be oblivious to the cold chills his touch brought to her fevered body.

"Mike, we both know I have little experience with men."

"But you have very sexy ribs." He shifted from her shoulder to his elbow and leaned over her once more.

"Even with six brothers, I don't know all that much."

"Mmm. Nice flat tummy."

"I never learned much, and I understand even less. I—uh—"

"Did you know that the curve of your hip fits my hand perfectly?"

"I'm not sure I even know—oh. . . ."

"Poor knee, does it hurt?"

"Nnno."

"There's a ridge here at your ankle. Is this where the break was?"

"Right, I mean left. Yes—no . . . I don't know."

"Jamie?"

"Yes?"

"I want you."

"Oh, Mike, please!" She moaned. "You promised you wouldn't hurry me."

"But I'm not, love. I only said that I wanted you. That's not pressure. You can wait until you're ready to tell me and I'll be as patient as Job."

"If you call what you're doing right this minute being patient, then one of us *is* crazy, and it *isn't* me."

"Nice ankles."

"Would you stop!"

"This knee has a scar too. Another strawberry?"

"You're ignoring me."

"No, I'm not."

"Then ignore me. Please."

"I don't think I've ever felt such smooth skin."

Jamie moved frantically, capturing the marauding hand that was poised just beneath her halter. In their embrace the fickle elastic had again betrayed her. The delicious undercurve of her small breasts was revealed to his appreciative eye. Even now, as she held tightly to his hand the tip of his thumb moved teasingly back and forth against her bare skin.

"I want you to stop this. I don't like it."

"Who're you trying to convince? If you hated it so much, why did it take so long to stop me?"

"I tried."

"No, you didn't."

"But I asked you to stop."

"You didn't mean it."

"I did!" she asserted strongly.

"No, Jamie. If you had, you would've done it long ago."

Her temper flashed into life. "You and your damn logic make me sooo damn mad!"

"Not mad. Let me show you." She only had time to see the laughter that was glinting in his eyes in the second before his lips brushed hers. Once, lightly, then deepening as she caught fire, responding as he had known she would. The carefully banked fires flared as she buried her hands in the shining thickness of his hair.

"Whatcha doin'?" The small voice sounded at Mike's shoulder. There, sitting cross-legged on the uneven boards, was Sam, a curious expression on his innocent face.

"Ahh, Sam." Mike rolled away from Jamie. "Are you sure your name isn't Herman?"

Childish laughter rang through the trees. "You jus' teasing. Me Sam." The child thumped his chest, then grew solemn as he remembered the purpose of his errand. "Uncle Jamie, Uncle Scott and Uncle Steve said for you to come play football. They need a quarter."

"Sure, Sam." With an effort Jamie roused herself from the dreamy mood that had captured her. "You run along and tell them I'm coming. Be careful going down the ladder. You know you're not supposed to climb up here alone."

"Not alone. You here."

The childish reasoning brought a smile to Jamie's lips. "You know what I mean. Now, do as I say, and be careful."

"Awright." Sam scrambled down the ladder, his tongue tucked in the corner of his mouth, as he gave the journey down his serious attention.

Only after the child had disappeared over the side of the treehouse did Jamie make an attempt to straighten her clothing. She tugged furtively at the loose halter, determined to ignore the gleam of barely suppressed interest that hovered in Mike's eyes. Despite Sam's timely interruption, he looked inordinately pleased with himself.

"Uncle Jamie, when you coming?" Sam's young voice rose from the base of the tree.

"*Uncle* Jamie?" Mike whispered for her ears only.

"Don't laugh. He has so many uncles and so few aunts, he gets us confused."

"In a few years he'll know the difference," Mike promised, his look sweeping Jamie's body with wicked satisfaction.

"Hurry, Uncle Jamie."

"Coming right now, Sam." She scrambled over the edge in much the same manner as the child had done. She landed gracefully by his side and waited for Mike to descend.

"Whatcha doin' up there with Mike, Uncle Jamie?"

"Your Uncle Jamie and I were solving some problems, Sam." Mike stood by the child. His shirt was respectably rebuttoned.

"Was it fun?"

"Nah. I'm glad you saved me."

"Saved you?" Sam giggled up at the tall man. "How?"

"I hate to admit this, but I've just discovered I'm not as tough as Uncle Jamie."

"Aww." Disbelief filled Sam's young face.

"It's true, cross my heart. That's a rough treehouse.

At first I thought Uncle Jamie must have a cast-iron behind, but it's too soft. So now I've decided she's just tougher than me. Why, your grandma said she's been sitting up there for hours. But look." He caressed the softly rounded curve of her bottom, ignoring her glare and her yelp of outrage. "See? No splinters. What did I tell you? She's one tough lady."

"Wait till I tell Daddy!" Sam whirled to race through the trees. "Daddy, Daddy. Uncle Jamie has a cast-iron behind but it's too soft and doesn't get splinters. That's why she's tougher than Mike and can sit in the treehouse longer."

"Big mouth," Jamie muttered when she heard the low rumbling of her brothers' laughter following Sam's enthusiastic report. "Now you've done it, you sharp-talking, slick-thinking—"

"Wonderful, sweet, lovable nuisance?"

"Yes, that's it, nuisance. Thank you."

"Maybe someday you'll get it all right." He breathed a mock sigh. "But you're welcome anyway. We'd better go or it's going to be too dark for this football game. I take it you're the quarter they need."

"Yeah, that's me," she acknowledged as they moved through the shaded walk back to the lawn. The choosing of the teams was already underway when they joined the waiting group.

"I get Jamie," Steve called.

"No fair. You had her last time." This from Scott, the leader of the opposing team.

"I did not."

It was a long-standing argument between the twins, accompanied by casual, teasing remarks from the rest of the family. Mike had met them earlier, before joining Jamie at the creek. They had, with their customary ease, accepted him as her friend, without question.

"How was the tree-sitting today, runt?" This from Andrew.

"Did you solve the problems of the world? Or more important, did you solve yours?" Alex delivered this comment cloaked under the guise of a jest, but Jamie knew he was deadly serious. Alex was the most sensitive of her brothers. His teasing was always more gentle, his concerns more obvious.

"While you boys are scrabbling around to see who gets Jamie, you might consider Mike as a choice player," Seth remarked, adding his two cents to the escalating argument between the twins.

"Sure, he played football for Tech," Simon reminded them. "That's what I call a tough man."

"No, that's not what makes him tough," Seth countered. "In my book, he's tough because he's the only male, ever, to successfully approach our little sister when she's in her sanctuary. I know I never would. I'd be afraid of losing my head."

Simon examined Mike closely. "Now that you mention it, he doesn't seem to have any claw marks. Do you suppose he tamed the spitfire?"

"If you don't hush, Simon, I'll show you spitfire!" Jamie promised with undisguised annoyance in her eyes. "Who's team is Smarty on? I want the other team. I'll settle his hash on the football field."

"Ha! Promises, promises." Simon threw an affectionate arm about his sister, who smiled in spite of herself. "It's trite, but true. Dynamite does come in small packages. Better beware, Mike."

"I intend to."

"I say we let Jamie decide," Steve interjected into Mike and Simon's banter. "What team did you play for last time?"

Jamie thought for a minute, then shook her head. "I really don't remember."

"How about if we flip for her?" Scott drew a coin from his pocket. "Heads I win, tails you lose."

"Funny! That one came over on the *Mayflower*. I call heads." Steve watched as the coin was flipped high in the air and landed at his feet. "Heads! I win, you lose. Next time, little brother, show more respect for your elders. Remember, I was there when you were born."

"Don't remind me. And to think I had considered forgiving Mom for having you at the same time she had me."

"Sour grapes, kid. Come on, Jamie, you're mine." Steve led his team to the far side of the lawn.

"Okay, Mike, I guess that means I get you." Scott motioned for his players to follow and huddle around him. "I hope you're as good as an ex-Tech man ought to be. Whoever gets Jamie always wins, so we have our work cut out for us."

The next few minutes were an eye-opener for Mike. He had assumed that even though it was a game of touch, there would be concessions made for Jamie. Not only for her femininity, but for her diminutiveness as well. But there were none. It was a give-and-take contest with all their natural sibling rivalry coming to the fore. Jamie guided her team with agile footwork and an accurate passing arm; she was the center of the game. As they dashed about—slipping, sliding, and often stumbling—the contest grew even more spirited, and Mike cringed at the risks she took. Far more often than not, she was in the middle of any heap, her lack of size forgotten in the sheer exuberance of the game.

As the end drew near the score was tied. In a quarterback sneak Jamie raced to the opposing team's imaginary goal line. Very fleet of foot, she wound around her large brothers, dodging and dancing, laughing as she ran. In desperation Scott, a man of over six feet, lunged instinctively at her. He hit her far harder than he intended and landed across her unprotected body. The loud whoosh of the breath being knocked from her was followed by eerie silence broken only by the distressed cry that broke from Mike's lips.

"Jamie!" He raced to her side, shoving Scott roughly from her. "Oh, God, sweetheart, are you hurt?"

Jamie rolled over onto her back, looking up with puzzled eyes at the man who was kneeling over her. With an effort she regained her breath. "For heaven's sake, Mike. Of course, I'm all right." She began to wheeze in a caricature of laughter. "Tell me, did I score?"

"Dammit, Jamie! That big ox could have broken your neck, and you want to know if you scored? What kind of crazy family is this?" In his agitation he didn't realize that his remarks might be considered insulting to her family. "Get your things. I'm taking you home."

"You're the one who's crazy." She sat up, one arm

propped on her raised knee. "What makes you think I'm going anywhere with you?"

"Because I said so." He rose to his feet. Turning to the group gathered about the two of them, he addressed the elder Brents. "I thank you for your hospitality, Mrs. Brent, Mr. Brent, but I do think it's time Jamie and I were leaving." Abruptly he turned back to Jamie, informed her he would be waiting in his car, and stalked from the yard.

The Brent family—mother, father, sons, and wives—watched in awe. No one spoke until Alex broke the silence. "Wow! He's got it bad, hasn't he?"

"Looks like it," drawled Andrew.

"I thought he was going to bash me one."

"He came close."

"Jamie." Carol's voice was gentle. "I think maybe you'd better go with him. Run get your things and don't worry about your car. One of your brothers will drop it off later."

A totally perplexed Jamie rose, brushing the damp grass from her shorts and halter. Resolutely she pulled the halter back down, thinking incongruously that she must remember to replace the elastic.

"Baby"—Larry Brent's voice was as gentle as his wife's had been—"your mother's right. All this is too new to him, and he's hurting. Go with him."

Jamie could only shake her head in confusion. She lightly kissed her parents and crossed the lawn, waving good-bye to her brothers and their wives as she went. Quickly she ran up the stairs, threw her clothes into the disreputable duffel, and left the house to join Mike in his car.

She slid into the seat at his side, but did not speak; neither did he. They drove across town, and in the silence her rage grew with each memory of his imperious commands.

"You acted like a fool, you know."

"How is it foolish to be concerned that you might be hurt?" The rough rasp of his words told her that he was as angry as she.

"I've been taking care of myself for a long time. I don't need you to be concerned about me."

"I think you do. That big lug could've killed you. Not one of them treated you gently. They knocked you about as hard as they did each other. They seemed to forget that you're a woman, and a very small one at that."

"I certainly hope so. I've spent my whole life proving to them that I could compete and I'd have been madder than hell if they'd dared pussyfoot around me. *That* would've been the final insult."

Mike didn't answer for a long while and Jamie thought the matter was resolved. She was still angry, but willing to let it cool.

"Tell me what you're trying to prove, and to whom?" The question startled her from her tense silence.

"I just told you what I *have* proved," she snapped, anger blazing again.

"No, you just told me what you thought you proved."

"Look, I only came with you because Mom and Dad thought I should. I don't want or need your analysis of my motives, or my successes and failures. I don't want to hear it, period!"

"You're going to hear it whether you want to or not," he snarled, sparing her not even a glance. "I watched you today. You were right in the middle of every fracas, acting like you were just as tough and just as big as your brothers. But you're not, and you never will be. I don't understand this need to compete with men. But, honey, if you have to, you've picked the wrong battlefield. You'll never be a tall strapping man no matter how hard you try, so why not accept yourself and make the most of the weapons you have?"

"You're talking nonsense. You just don't understand."

"No. *You* don't understand. You don't understand that you have a heart-stopping smile. You don't understand that with your soft, husky voice you could reduce the strongest of men to mindless idiots. Instead, you compete on *their* terms, on *their* grounds. Is that really what you want? Be careful what you ask for in life, Jamie, you might just get it. Are you sure you want the cold, empty life of constant competition? Or would you rather be a woman?"

"I've already tried that and what did it get me? Or have you forgotten the mistake I made?"

"I haven't forgotten a thing. You were a child then, playing at being an adult, and yes, you made a mistake."

"Twenty is hardly a child." She sighed, tired of the old story.

"I don't care how old you were, you were still a child. Now you're a grown woman, with mature wisdom and much to offer, if you will."

"We've already established that I don't know how." A sharp edge of sarcasm gave her words an alien self-mockery.

"And I've offered more than once to help."

"No thanks. After today I think you're too dangerous for me. If I let you, you could become too important in my life."

"Coming from you, that's quite an admission, but we no longer have a choice, honey. We're going to be lovers; it's in the cards." His anger had gone suddenly and completely, replaced by a tender teasing.

"I don't want a lover," Jamie said flatly.

"Neither do I. At least not only a lover. I want a friend, a partner. And when we're alone, I want a woman who knows who she is, what she is, and is proud of it. When you become that woman, our loving will be unquenchable. In the meantime I'll just hang around and be your friend."

"I'd rather you go away."

"Have you forgotten? I can't go, I'm yours."

"Don't start."

"Anyway, I have to be here to guide our daughter. She must be cherished and taught to be all the woman she can be."

"What daughter?"

"The one we're going to have, with black hair like yours and maybe green eyes like mine. She'll be breathtaking."

"You aren't going away, are you?" she asked evenly, her expression strained.

"Nope."

• • • •

He was there. The previous day might never have happened, and her angry words never said. He was impervious to her insults as well as her wishes. Yesterday had almost been her undoing, for in the heat of anger she had given him more ammunition in his battle. She thought again how foolish she had been to admit he could become too important to her.

With a nervous flourish she parked the VW in its space and slid out. Even as the door was shutting, she turned to face him, striving to maintain her composure. She swept him with an assessing look, trying to deny how attractive he was, leaning there against the strong supports of the garage. In his position of repose he was huge and overwhelmingly handsome in a three-piece soft-brown suit. A stray lock of shining hair fell over his forehead and in fierce anger at herself she fought the desire to smooth it back.

" 'Morning, honey." His soft voice was a caress and suddenly her knees grew weak.

"I asked you to go away," she said quietly, annoyed at herself for her uncontrollable reaction to the sound of his voice. This was stupid! How could she let a man, any man, do this to her? She drew herself up, ignoring how her body ached from the rigid posture. Every muscle in her body was taut as she willed herself not to tremble.

"I meant it when I asked you to go away."

"Did you?" He straightened away from the post that should have appeared massive, but didn't because of his own great size. In a step he towered over her in the shadowed parking deck. "I don't remember."

"You should. I certainly made it clear enough."

She flinched as his hands came down on her shoulders to hold her in a gentle prison.

"Sorry, sweetheart, but all I can remember is how beautiful you were waking, warm and drowsy, in the sunlight. I remember how you kissed me—"

"I never—"

"How you touched me with those maddening hands."

"I didn't—"

"I remember how your hair curled around your breast, inviting my touch."

"No—"

"I remember how smooth your skin is, and the soft sweet curve of your body moist from the heat, when you let that scrap of a halter slip."

"Let it slip!"

"I remember how I ached to kiss each droplet away."

"Oh, rats!" She swayed involuntarily, knees growing weaker.

"I remember"—it was his arms that held her prisoner now—"how you shivered when I touched you like this." His breath was warm as he bent to nip at the lobe of her ear. "And this." He took the soft flesh into his mouth and tugged gently.

"Please."

"Please what, sweetheart?"

"Please stop," she whispered into his chest. "You must!"

"Why must I?" From the hoarseness in his voice, she knew he was suffering as she was.

"Because I can't stand anymore. This is madness." Her own voice was trembling.

"If this is madness, then I thank God for it."

"Can't you be serious for even a minute?" She pushed ineffectually against his hard chest.

"It's no fun being serious. I'd much rather laugh and be happy making wild, passionate love to you."

"In a parking deck?" she managed breathlessly.

"Ah-ha! You have a better place in mind?"

"No, of course not."

"Then you want me to make love to you here." His head again swooped low, seeking her lips.

"No!" Swiftly she turned her head, and his warm lips grazed across her cheek, leaving a trail of fire. "I don't want you to make love to me here or anyplace. I don't want you to make love to me at all."

"Poor little sweetheart, you do insist on fooling yourself, don't you? Only seconds ago I was making love to you here in this parking deck and could have in any other place you might name—and you did want it."

"No! No! No! Please, no! I don't want you! I don't! You . . . you . . . you're a supercilious, annoying, persistent . . . persistent—"

"Sexy, irresistible, gorgeous fool?"

"Yes, gorgeous fool. Thank you."

"At least you got a little more of it right this time. Maybe next time will be the charm, and you're welcome."

"You make me so angry!" Jamie's hands were curled into the lapels of his jacket. She stood within the circle of his arms as they linked loosely about her. She spoke in bewildered agitation as she looked up at him. "You can let me go now."

"You were free to go any time you wished, Jamie. All you had to do was step away. But ask yourself: did you truly want to? Don't you like being in my arms as much as I like holding you?"

The truth of what he said hit Jamie with the impact of a blow. His embrace had offered a comfort and security that she found almost irresistible. Even now she wanted to step closer, to lean against him, to rest and forget all but him. Startled by the direction of her thoughts, she turned in his arms with catlike grace and pushed them away in one smooth motion. The rapid beat of her heels on the concrete was the only sound. One unfortunate glance over her shoulder at the smiling man who watched her only added fuel to the fire of her angry frustration.

He stood there in the gloom of the cavernous recesses, a satisfied smile lighting his face. He knew that he had once again broken down her defenses and drawn from her a response, however reluctant. He watched her silently, then moved out of the shadows.

Chapter Seven

As she moved down the ramp onto the street, the beat of her heels no longer echoed and her step slowed as did the ragged beat of her heart. She had begun to regain her normal stride and was approaching Bill McClain when a heavy arm fell across her shoulders, long fingers curling around her bare arm.

" 'Mornin', Bill." It was Mike's deep voice rather than her own greeting the dark, friendly man. She shut her mouth with a snap, her eyes flashing fire at the hand that rested possessively at her elbow.

"Hi, Brad. Missed you last week, Jamie." Bill smiled at her, not missing the significance of the hand Mike was moving up and down her arm in a caress. It was the brand of possession, the stamp of ownership.

A twinkle of male understanding gleamed in Bill's eyes as he asked, "Did you have a good vacation?"

"Yes, thank you." This terse sentence was all she could manage as her anger turned to embarrassed rage.

"It was better than good, honey. It was great. Especially yesterday." With a chuckle, Mike dropped a kiss on her forehead.

"*If* you don't mind, I'd like to get on to the office." Her stony stare made a mockery of the purr in her voice, as she looked into his teasing eyes, promising herself sweet revenge.

"Sure, honey. See you later, Bill."

Jamie stalked away, looking neither right nor left, not daring to allow herself a glimpse of him for fear the seething rage within her would erupt. He had caused enough of a scene with his recent antics. She would not add fuel to the gossip. They were beyond the hearing of Bill when his hand at her arm halted her in her tracks.

"Are you angry, honey?"

"Don't you honey me!" She pulled her arm from his grasp. "You've sprinkled that word around enough for one day. How dare you do and say the things you did in front of him? Now he's sure to think there's something between us."

"Of course he will, because there is." His smug smile was maddening.

"There is *not*, and even if there were, after today there wouldn't be." Even to Jamie the words were nonsensical.

"Now, now, honey—er, Jamie. Let's not have a lovers' quarrel here in the street."

"Lovers' quarrel!" she shrieked. "This is not a quarrel, lover or otherwise. This is war! You're going to be sorry you ever met me!"

"Never. Nothing you could ever do would make me sorry we met. Let's face it, if it weren't for you I might be dead or at least seriously injured."

"Before I'm through with you, you just might wish that can had hit you."

"Ah, now, what could a little thing like you do to a giant like me?"

Jamie had begun to walk away with determined steps, steps that he easily matched. Now she slowed, stopped, and turned to face him. "You'll just have to wait and see. But remember, there is no rage like that of a woman angered."

His laughter filled the street, leaving Jamie to blink in perturbed surprise. "*Scorned*, honey, the word is *scorned*. And even with your fractured proverbs and gorgeous, flaming temper, you'll never be scorned. But I await your vengeance with great relish!"

"Blast you!" She wheeled on her heel and began for the fourth time her journey to work.

"Hey, wait a minute." His hand on her arm slowed but did not stop her. "Is that all?"

"All what?"

"Aren't you going to try to call me any names?"

"Oh, but I did." She smiled sweetly at him.

"You did?"

"Yes, beautiful ones. Names that fit you perfectly."

"What were they?" He grinned adding to her anger.

"Never mind. They're all right here." She tapped

her temple with a slender finger. "Up here, you're quite accurately cataloged."

"If you want to call me little love names, Jamie, you can. I'd like to hear endearments on your lips.

"They are not endearments. You wouldn't like them."

"I doubt you could remember any really terrible names," he said with barely concealed laughter.

He was teasing her and she knew it. It had become a habit for him, a way of working through her tensions and drawing a laugh or a smile from her. But this time she refused to fall into his scheme. In her irritation she wanted to lash out at him.

"Look, Mike," she began, far more calmly than she really felt, "I'm starting to feel like a butterfly stuck to flypaper. Everywhere I turn, you're there. It's almost as if I have two shadows now. You're crowding me and you're rushing me. I can't think straight. Whenever you're in arm's length of me, you're holding me and kissing me—and that makes matters worse. Can't you back off a bit and quit playing the male chauvinist? Can't you let up on this . . . this sexual harassment?"

Mike's hand clamped suddenly, tightly, around her elbow, drawing her into the darkness of a doorway. His eyes had become slits of green ice beneath the gold-tipped lashes. The low rasp of his voice held the cutting edge of anger. "It would seem I've underestimated you. That was a vicious thing to say. Perhaps you'd better explain."

The minute she had flung the words at him, Jamie wished she could recall them. Startled by his intense response, she regretted even more her childish need for revenge. She regretted her actions, but refused to give him the satisfaction of an apology. With forced bravado she spoke in even tones. "You keep hammering away at me to use my quote, 'womanly power,' unquote. That, Mr. Bradford, sounds suspiciously like you're suggesting I use sex to get where and what I desire. I find the idea both belittling and distasteful. I have a mind that serves my purposes nicely. I don't need to trade on my body."

Mike drew in a deep breath, his fingers bit even deeper into the soft flesh of her arm. In controlled rage he spoke quiet words that slashed at her as he swept her with eyes filled with cold pity.

"You little fool. Are you stupid or are you being deliberately obtuse? I've not once suggested that kind of prostitution to you. What I've asked is that you be all you can be—whether it's a hard driving career *person*, wife, or mother, or all three. Tell me, is femininity a crime? Does it make you inferior? Is that what you think? If so, my dear little idiot, then it is you who are the chauvinist, not I."

The lazy, teasing drawl she had become accustomed to was nothing like this cold disgust. Jamie made a futile gesture of entreaty in a clumsy attempt to appease him. Every word he said was true. She had simply lashed out in blind, childish anger, spewing out thoughtless words.

He ignored the slight move she made toward him as the expression on his ashen face grew even colder. "I haven't asked you to be less, but more. I only want you to remember what you are and to be proud of it. You can be all things and still be a woman. But you have to accept the limitations imposed on you by your size and by your gender." The last word was a sarcastic slur, as though he avoided the mention of sex and all it might imply. "Concentrate on your assets within those limitations and you'll be stronger. Be anything, be everything, but for God's sake, Jamie, be a woman."

He dropped his hand from hers, speaking again before she could think to answer his charges. "This is neither the time nor the place for this discussion. I'll be out of town until Wednesday, but I'll come by your place when I get back. We'll settle this once and for all. Have a good day, Jamie."

She caught one final glimpse of his carefully blank face, then stared unbelievingly as he walked away from her. As she watched him move with his confident step she felt the first deep twinge of unease that perhaps he was walking out of her life. This time forever.

"Well, Jamie," she said aloud, "It was what you wanted, wasn't it? You didn't want anyone—man or woman—upsetting your well-ordered life." Feeling coldly and terribly isolated, she moved from the doorway. She had taken several steps before realizing she had been standing in the entrance of the Bradford Building. With the ache of unshed tears constricting her throat she turned to push open the heavy door.

"Good morning, Miss Brent."

"Good morning, Mr. Hanson." Head down, the subdued Jamie missed the alarmed frown that crinkled the kindly old face as faded eyes watched her enter the elevator.

•   •   •

"Anybody for lunch?" Meg's red curls bobbed around the partially opened door.

"None for me, thanks." Jamie stretched as she dropped her pen from cramped fingers. "I want to finish this translation while I have it fresh in my mind."

"Come on, Jamie. You never eat lunch anymore. The cafeteria's bad, but surely you don't plan to starve in order to avoid it. At least keep me company and watch me while I flirt with ptomaine. While I eat you can tell me about your vacation. Please. . . ." Meg produced her most beguiling grin, allowing the dimple that deeply marked her right cheek to grow even deeper. Golden brown eyes pleaded prettily as heavy lashes fluttered down to brush smooth cheeks.

"Meg Lawson, you're impossible." Jamie exploded into laughter. "Don't waste all that charm on me. Save it for some poor unsuspecting man. Flutter those beautiful lashes at him, and he'll—" Jamie stopped short as she realized what she was saying.

"Jamie?"

"Uh . . . Meg, I was only joking. But . . . do you really do that? I mean, do you really—you know."

"You mean, do I play that little act for real? The answer's no, Jamie. I wouldn't think of it. I couldn't get away with the coy sex-kitten act and I wouldn't want to. But I'm a woman and I never let a man forget it."

Jamie looked at the woman in front of her. Meg was not beautiful, but she had an aura of confidence that made her arrestingly attractive. She had a sharp mind that she never bothered to hide and a razor-edged wit that entertained but never cut. Meg teased about an uninteresting social life, but Jamie knew that

since their college days that had never been the case
except by choice. Perhaps there was much she could
learn from her friend.

"I think I will join you for lunch after all." Jamie
smiled, rising to join Meg at the door.

There was a general exodus from the offices with
the greater part of the group headed for the cafeteria.
Covertly Jamie watched as Meg gracefully accepted
courtesy after courtesy, bestowing her beautiful smile
in return.

"So that's how it's done," Jamie muttered later,
seated at a small table, a glass of iced tea in her hand.

"How what's done?" Meg asked curiously.

"I've been told by an expert that I don't use my
womanly wiles. In all the time I've known you, I've
never realized before what a performance you give."

"It's not a performance, Jamie," Meg answered
mildly, not taking offense. "I enjoy the small courtesies.
It makes me feel more a woman."

"And the man?"

"It keeps him more aware of the differences between us. If it gives him pleasure to show me those
kindnesses as simply a friend or a gentleman, it doesn't
make me any less a person to accept them gracefully.
A small courtesy and a pleasant smile can brighten any
day."

"Is that all there is to it?"

"Of course not. There are many kinds of relation-
ships and in each we act accordingly. In a special relationship between a man and a woman—"

"By 'special' you mean lovers," Jamie interjected
bluntly.

"Yes, I do, Jamie." Meg continued calmly, ignoring her friend's scowling face. "There are special courtesies and pleasures that are apart from the world. If I had a lover and I wanted to please him in the countless ways lovers do, how does it diminish me? How can I hurt myself by reminding him that he's a man and I'm a woman?"

"And it all starts by letting a man open the door for you," Jamie drawled sarcastically.

"Well," Meg giggled in spite of herself, "It's a start."

"So the next man I meet, I let him hold a door for me—and heaven knows where it might lead." The scowl disappeared from Jamie's face as she convulsed into giggles. "I'd guess I'd better make sure it's not a bedroom door."

" *That* depends on the man, the circumstances, and how you feel about him. Suppose the man were Mike?"

Jamie sobered suddenly. "I don't think that's a problem I'll be having."

"You haven't seen him since your vacation?"

"Oh, sure, I saw him yesterday and again this morning."

"Then did you talk?"

"When we're together, we don't exactly talk. I stutter around, while he—Well, anyway, I can't seem to get out a coherent sentence when I'm with him. Then I spend the next few hours talking to *myself.*"

"I get the picture." Meg laughed. "I can't think of but one other man I'd rather *not* talk to."

"Who might that be?" Jamie's interest was piqued.

"Never mind. That's another story. I'll tell you some time." Meg brushed aside her question. "Now, what is it you say in these conversations you carry on with yourself?"

"They're usually about Mike."

"I thought as much. You've got it bad, haven't you?"

"It?"

"You're in love with him."

"Fat lot of good it does me," Jamie said miserably, not bothering to deny her love.

Meg studied her friend's morose face. "You haven't quarreled, have you?"

"Violently."

"Oh, Jamie, you don't want to lose him."

"He's not mine to lose. Haven't you seen the ring he wears?"

"The sapphire?"

"Yes. It's obviously very important to him."

"I'd never noticed it until I heard a stenographer ask him about it."

"What did he say?" Jamie tensed, dreading the answer.

"He said it belonged to a very dear friend."

"So! You see, that tells you where I stand with him. This dear friend is someone he wants to be reminded of constantly."

"Good grief, Jamie! If the ring bothers you, ask the man about it."

"I can't." Jamie looked down in misery at her own bare fingers.

"Look," Meg began patiently, "it makes no sense to worry over something that may be of no consequence. Maybe the ring is his grandmother's, his mother's, or—"

"His lover's," Jamie supplied quietly.

"I don't think so. I know from all the gossip that he's seen any number of women over the years, but they were never more than casual dates. None of them ever lasted long enough to be more."

"He could have had a romance you don't know about."

"We both know he could, but I really don't think so. Ask him about the damn ring," Meg urged again.

"I doubt I'll get the chance after this morning."

Meg set her glass down and folded her napkin, watching the fresh wave of misery in her friend's face. "What did you quarrel about?" she asked softly.

"It was a doozy."

"Oh, dear, what happened?"

"I said some awful things and called him a male chauvinist and accused him of sexual harassment."

Meg moaned. "You didn't."

"I'm afraid I did. Frankly I didn't expect the reaction I got. Most men laugh it off or are even proud of the label."

"Mike Bradford wouldn't be."

"So I found out." Jamie grimaced. "His reaction was extreme."

"You don't know about his father?" Meg leaned back in her chair, intrigued by the emotions that were crossing Jamie's face.

"How could I? Until you wrote me about this job six months ago, I was buried in the French countryside, remember?"

"I guess I wasn't thinking. It got so much publicity here, I assumed you'd heard about it from someone. Jamie, just before he died, Mike's father was involved in a particularly ugly lawsuit. The charge was sexual harassment."

"Oh, no. What have I done?" The eyes that stared at Meg were dark with pain.

Meg reached out to hold Jamie's trembling hand tenderly.

Jamie had been back from a lunch she couldn't eat for more than twenty minutes and still had not returned to the translation on her desk. In the past she had been able, through dogged stubbornness, to channel her thoughts. But, devastated by what she had learned from Meg, she had spent two miserable days unable to think of anything but Mike and the hurt she had caused him. She sat idly, tapping her pen against her desk, her mind frozen by the cold recognition of her own foolishness.

"Dammit, Jamie!" She threw the pen down in disgust. "You acted like an utter idiot, a mewling spoiled child. Good grief! How could you do such a thing? Ignorance is no excuse."

The telephone on her desk rang, breaking noisily into her mutterings. She glared at the offending instrument. Bent on self-castigation, she wanted no interruptions as she applied the whip to her conscience. The phone rang again and she could not ignore its intrusion.

"Idiot!" she admonished herself. "Stop wallowing in self-pity and answer the stupid thing."

For a split second longer she delayed answering the call. Finally, strangely reluctant, she lifted the receiver. Her voice was strained, hardly sounding like her own. "Jamie Brent's office."

"Jamie?"

"Mike!" There were only the hollow sounds of an open line as Jamie struggled for words. Suddenly she became aware that she could hear noises that surged in waves in the background. "Where are you?"

"I'm in the lobby of the conference center in Charlotte. My meeting here is running a bit longer than I expected. I can't say when it'll be over." Mike paused as if planning his next words. "I'd still like to come by when I get back."

"Tonight?"

"Yes, tonight." His voice grew strained. "Do you have other plans?"

"No. No plans. It's just that I thought you might be too tired after the conference and the long drive back."

"I won't be driving back, Jamie. A friend will be giving me a lift in her plane. I should see you sometime about midnight."

"All right, Mike."

"Honey—" What he had meant to say was interrupted by a definitely feminine purr, sounding loud and clear over the line before Mike muffled the receiver with his hand. Then he must have moved it away, for Jamie heard quite clearly the rest of the husky-voiced conversation.

"Mike, darling, if you don't come on, we'll miss the first part of the meeting."

"I'll be along as soon as I can, Clarice." His voice

was weak as he spoke away from the instrument, then grew stronger as he turned back again to speak to Jamie. "Sorry, honey, I've got to run. See you tonight, hopefully no later than midnight."

The loud drone of the dial tone signaled he had hung up without ceremony. Jamie sat frowning at the receiver as if it could answer the questions that were filling her mind. Who was Clarice with the sexy voice? And the friend with the plane? Had the sapphire ring belonged to either? As soon as the thoughts occurred, Jamie put them aside. Mike had spoken to her of trust, and she found that she did trust and believe in him.

By ten o'clock Jamie was already pacing the floor. In the last five minutes she had looked at the clock as many times. The apartment was quite cool, but there were beads of moisture on her forehead. Impatiently she wiped them away with a damp hand.

"This is ridiculous," she scolded herself. "It's over two hours before he's due back and already you're beside yourself. At this rate, idiot, you're going to be a foot shorter and too exhausted to talk to the man."

Whirling, she paced to the sofa and sank down into its soft cushions. Her restless hand strayed to the latest issue of a glossy magazine lying unopened on the table before her. As she flipped uninterestedly through the pages, turning rapidly back to front, one picture arrested her gaze. It was the photograph of a tall brown-haired man who stared soulfully at the camera with brilliant green eyes.

"Green eyes," she muttered, unaware that she had spoken aloud. The magazine sailed across the room and Jamie was once more on her feet. From the sofa to the terrace, from the terrace to the kitchen door, back and forth she paced. Tonight she was dressed in a cotton sundress. Thin straps held the bodice of cobweb lace, and the soft, pliant fabric clung closely to her body. From within the thigh-high slit, the same lace caressed her slim leg with each step as she strode unceasingly back and forth. Her feet were bare, for the matching sandals were tucked beneath the sofa's edge where she had left them after her last foray.

The shrill peal of the telephone brought her pacing to a sharp halt. She stood breathless while it rang once, twice, three times. After the third ring she moved quickly to snatch the receiver from its cradle.

"Hello."

"Jamie? You sound strange. Is anything wrong?" Carol Brent's voice forced her back to some semblance of sanity.

"No, Mom. Nothing's wrong, I'm fine."

"You're sure?"

"Positive. What can I do for you?"

"I called about the picnic this weekend. Your dad and I thought it would be nice if you brought Mike."

"Mike? No, I don't think so. Anyway, I'm sure he'll have other plans." She couldn't ask him. She couldn't risk the rebuff; it would be too painful.

"It won't hurt to ask him, Jamie. He can always say no if it doesn't fit into his schedule."

"He's awfully busy." Jamie hedged, plucking nervously at the twisted cord.

"Had you rather I ask him?"

"No, Mom." Jamie sighed, defeated by her mother's insistence. "I'll ask him."

"There's just one more thing. Be sure to tell him the ground rules for this picnic—there will be positively no touch football." Carol chuckled.

"That sounds like a winner," Jamie agreed firmly, then panicked as the doorbell rang, its musical notes reverberating through the quiet of her apartment. "Mom, there's someone at the door. I'll call you tomorrow."

Not waiting for a reply, Jamie hung up. Slowly she walked to the door, pausing before the small mirror in the foyer to check her loose hair and minimal makeup. She licked her dry lips, then, squaring her shoulders, turned the lock and opened the door.

"I know it's late, but I didn't think you would be in bed yet."

"Mrs. Horton! How are you? I mean, won't you come in?" Jamie paused in frustration, searching for words to hide her disappointment.

"No, dear, I really can't stay. I have only a minute. I'm baking cookies and thought you might like some." A plate of warm, deliciously fragrant cookies, accompanied by a shy smile, were placed in Jamie's hand. "I hope you enjoy them."

"You shouldn't have bothered." It was all Jamie could think to say.

"It was no bother." An ancient hand patted her cheek. "Good night, my dear."

"Good night, Mrs. Horton, and thank you." She closed the door softly and with an effort shook off the feeling of depression that was assailing her as she took the cookies to the kitchen.

Abstractedly retracing her steps to the sofa, she bent to retrieve the magazine lying on the floor beside the fire screen. Sitting there huddled in the corner, she riffled through it until she found what she was seeking. Smoothing back the pages, she sat for a long time staring at the man with green eyes that were so like Mike's. A tentative finger stroked the sensual curve of firm lips, so like Mike's. In a trancelike motion she covered a curl that had fallen over the broad, dark forehead. Like Mike, and yet unlike him.

"This is stupid!" Again the magazine sailed through the room. "Here I am, a grown woman, mooning over a picture that looks only slightly like a man who has turned my life completely upside down."

Jamie was on her feet again. One of her long, hard strides took her near the magazine that rested halfway against a chair. One swift kick and it was shoved from sight.

"Blast and be damned, all green-eyed men! I won't let him upset me. I won't. I'm going to pull myself together, be charming, be calm and cool. I'll apologize for hurting him, then send him on his way. I'll—" She caught sight of herself in the mirror. Her face was flushed and her eyes were bright. In her wild striding her hair had tangled and fallen over one shoulder.

"Jamie," she said to her reflection, "you're a mess. Of course, it doesn't really matter since all you're going to do is send the man on his way, remember? Oh, drat! I'm talking to myself again. Jamie." She leaned forward to peer almost nearsightedly at her image. *"Shut up!"*

The decisive rap at the door cut into her rambling monologue. Her breathing quickened, then seemed to stop. Running an agitated hand over her tousled hair, she flew to the door. Stopping short, she made a valiant effort to control the swell of anticipation that was welling up inside her. With her shoulders rigidly straight, she extended an unsteady hand and turned the knob. An eternity passed before the lock disengaged and the heavy wood panel moved.

Chapter Eight

They stood on opposite sides of the open door. Neither spoke and neither looked away. The clock began to strike the hour. With each note Jamie's heart began to beat faster. At the strike of eleven, she found her voice.

"You're early."

"Yes."

"I didn't expect you so soon."

"Perhaps I should have waited until twelve."

"No. No, of course not. I'm glad you came early." Her voice trailed away and she was left with nothing to say. The ticking of the clock filled an empty silence.

"Eleven isn't exactly early," Mike ventured.

"No. No, I suppose it isn't."

"I would've come sooner, but this meeting was

one I couldn't miss." Tiredly he ran his hand over his face.

Jamie couldn't move. Her parched throat threatened to close. Unconsciously her gaze swept over him as he stood in the gloom of the dimly lit hallway. Never had he seemed so large, or so handsome. His eyes sparkled with a green fire and his golden-brown hair glistened as if just washed. The collar above his loosened tie framed the powerful column of his neck. Mesmerized, she touched her own throat and found that her pulse was pounding there with an erratic rhythm that quickened with a hunger that made her tremble. Feeling his eyes upon her, she dropped her hand away, letting it hang loosely at her side.

"Mike, I—" she began.

"Jamie—" he spoke at the same time.

"Sorry." He shoved his hands into his pockets, and Jamie was stunned to see that he was as nervous as she.

"What were you going to say?" she asked quietly.

"You first."

"No, really, I . . . I . . ." It was too much. The tensions of the day and her own remorse destroyed her valiant composure. A glittering tear spilled from her eye.

"Oh, God. Don't cry, honey." He reached for her, gathering her small body close. "Please don't cry."

"I'm sorry. I'm sorry. I'm sorry." The dam broke beneath her pent-up emotions, and she began sobbing into the softness of his silken shirt. "I never meant to hurt you."

Without releasing her, he tilted her head up with

one big hand. With a touch that was amazingly gentle he stroked away the tears with his thumb. "Don't you think I know that, Jamie? I'm the one who should be apologizing."

"No." She burrowed her face into his chest again. "I was ugly and mean and I wouldn't blame you if you never wanted to see me again."

"Never wanted to see you again?" He framed her face with his palms, his incredulous eyes burning into her. "You're all I could think about all day. I could hardly wait to get back here. Poor Clarice even missed her dinner because I was in such a rush. This is probably the last time she'll offer me a ride home from a business meeting."

"Clarice?" Jamie hiccuped, her tears beginning to dry on her cheeks.

"My aunt. As my father's only sister, she attends most business conferences. Mainly to keep an eye on me, I think."

"Poor Clarice, she must be starving." Happily Jamie settled deeper into Mike's arms.

"Honey?"

"Mmm?"

"I think we should go inside. The hall's not exactly the place for what I have in mind."

"Ohmigosh!" Jamie pulled away, her face flaming. "What would the peanut gallery think if they should see us?"

"Mrs. Horton already did." He chuckled and with an easy push directed her into the foyer.

"Mike . . ." she began.

"Jamie . . ." Again at the same time he spoke.

Both paused, and this time both laughed. "You first." Mike repeated.

"No," she said firmly. "You first this time."

"We do need to talk." He brushed her hair from her shoulders and buried his hands in the dark silk.

"I know." Jamie nodded, her voice an unsteady whisper. "We've needed to for a long time."

"Jamie." Only her name, nothing more. He drew her back into his arms. Holding her closely, he stood not speaking, nor making any move to deepen the embrace.

For a short time she succumbed to the heady maleness of him. His was an overwhelming charm, a charisma against which she had no defense, now or ever. Desperately she fought to gather her wits about her. Slowly but determinedly, she drew away from him, dimly realizing that if they were to talk, she must keep him at arm's length.

"Mike, this isn't solving anything."

"Right. Pleasant as it is, we're avoiding the issue." Hesitantly he relinquished his hold on her and allowed her to slip away. As she moved farther into the room, his eyes followed her.

"Come, sit," she commanded, patting a plump pillow at the sofa's edge. "You look worse than exhausted."

"I think you're right. I passed exhaustion about three hours ago. I hope you realize, honey, that because of you I now have the reputation of being a slave driver." He sank down into the welcome comfort of the overstuffed cushion.

"Slave driver, perhaps, but never a chauvinist and

all the name implies," Jamie murmured in an agonized voice.

"Don't, Jamie." Mike's hand engulfed hers as he drew her nearer. When she stood between his knees, his free hand at her nape coaxed her lips to his for a tender kiss.

"No!" She recoiled from him. He watched her in surprise as she backed away, her hands extended before her. "We mustn't start that. If we do, we both know where it will lead."

"You're right." He sighed, his head dropping wearily back against the sofa. "If you'll get me a drink, we'll have that talk."

"One drink coming up." She laughed. Her bare feet made no sound on the carpet as she crossed to the liquor cabinet. Glad to have something to do with her hands, she smiled down at her newly acquired stock of Mike's favorite brand. Into a glass of ice she poured a small splash of whiskey, then added water in the proportion she had learned he liked.

"Mike."

"Mmm?" he answered, but his eyes remained closed.

"Your drink."

The heavy gold-tipped lashes swept up and his gaze moved leisurely over her body. The ice in the drink tinkled against the side of the glass as Jamie's hand shook under the intensity of his look. When he straightened and took the drink, his fingers brushed unsteadily against hers, lingering before moving away.

"Sit beside me, Jamie."

She refused with one sharp shake of her head.

Swiftly before she could change her mind, she stepped
to the far end and huddled into the corner of the sofa.
With her bare feet folded under her, she picked up a
throw pillow, holding it like a shield before her. She
rested her chin on its ruffled edge and regarded him
with wary eyes. She was fearful that he might pluck her
from her perch and by taking her in his arms, shatter
her hard-won composure.

"What're you doing way over there?" The question
was a low, irritated growl.

"You know we have to talk and we both know
that the only way we will is to keep some distance between us."

"Right again, honey." Mike drank sparingly from
the glass in his hand.

"Mike, I know about your father." She blurted it
out in a rush as her courage failed rapidly. She hated
the need to broach the painful subject. "Please believe
that I didn't know that morning."

"I know that now." He set the drink down on the
table. With his hands clasped and his elbows resting on
his knees, he pressed his eyes against his knuckles.
Quiet stretched between them, then he roused and
spoke. "I will admit I felt differently that morning. But
at the time I was too angry to think clearly, and I was
hurt."

He lifted his head. "I wouldn't have believed another human being could hurt me so."

"I know," Jamie murmured. "I saw it in your eyes.
That's why I couldn't blame you if you hated me."

"The most painful part"—Mike continued as if he
hadn't heard—"was that it was the sort of cruelty that

the Jamie Brent I thought I knew would never be capable of. I walked away from you because I had to. When the fog cleared and I could think rationally, I knew there must be some explanation. It was then I understood you knew nothing about the sordid hearing and my father's death."

"I didn't. At least not then." Her hands tightened around the pillow, but it was his contorted face she longed to touch. She wanted fiercely to smooth away the fatigue and the ache.

"Who told you?"

"Meg."

"What did she tell you?" His voice was raspy as though his throat hurt from the words.

"Only that he died in the midst of a lawsuit, and that the charge was sexual harassment." Jamie dropped her eyes, unable to match his hard stare. "Was it terrible?"

"Yes." He spoke bitterly. "Living it day-to-day, hearing the unfounded charges and accusations blown out of all sense of proportion, it was one of the ugliest things I've ever seen. If you'd known my father, you'd understand."

Mike's massive shoulders slumped beneath the burden of remembered sorrows. His words recalled for Jamie his own assurance that sharing pain could lessen the hurt. Who had shared this with him? Her eyes were drawn irresistibly from his face downward to his tightly closed fists. There, in its customary place, was the ring. By its very delicacy she knew it belonged to a very feminine woman. Who was she? What did she mean to Mike? And where was she now?

"Tell me about your father," she said softly, forcing all thoughts of the ring and the woman to whom it belonged from her mind.

"I'm not sure I can," he said, faltering. "He was the sort of man who defies description. If I told you what he was really like, I would sound like a hero-worshiping kid."

"Tell me, please," she urged, not only because she wanted to know, but because she could see Mike needed to talk. He, too, had a deep hurt that needed exorcising. Could she, by listening, ease it as he had hers?

The mellow tone of the grandfather clock, deep and low, sounded the half hour. The last note hovered in the dimly lit room, filling the expectant silence.

"Eleven thirty. I should go. Tomorrow's a working day and you need your rest," Mike said without moving.

"No." Jamie was quietly emphatic. "A few hours sleep, more or less, aren't important. The important thing is that I know about your father and understand how you felt about him."

"If you insist, Jamie," he capitulated. "But remember, I warned you: it isn't a pretty story." He took one more sip from the forgotten drink, set it down, then leaned his head back. A soft brown curl fell forward. Jamie resisted the nearly overpowering urge to tuck it back as he began to speak, his deep-timbred voice quiet but steady.

"Dad was a big man, almost exactly my size. He had no time for weight training and such, but he was the strongest man I've ever known. The combination of strength and size would have been frightening, except for his gentleness. It was beyond him to hurt any living thing. Size and strength can be a burden, and he felt the need to protect others, even from himself. He lived with the constant fear that he would inadvertently harm someone smaller or weaker. It was this attitude that shaped his life." Mike grew silent, his eyes remaining closed. Jamie waited patiently, the pillow still clutched before her.

"I don't fool myself that he couldn't be tough, or even mean, if the need arose. But that was a side my mother and I never saw. He was most protective of her. It was she he was proudest of—her mind and her kindness, as well as her beauty. He treated her as his partner and his love."

"It sounds like a wonderful marriage," Jamie said.

"It was. But Dad was trusting for a man of his time. He assumed all women were like Mother."

"To be trusted and cared for?"

"Yes. Michelle Harbison was beyond his understanding." He spat the name as if it were unpleasant on his tongue. "She knew something very few did. Dad couldn't handle alcohol. Two drinks and he was out." A bitter sound that had little to do with true laughter rumbled in his chest. "Surprising, isn't it, for one so large?"

"You drink very little."

Eyes, both blue and green turned to the half-filled glass before him. Mike shifted to an erect position, leaning his head on his clasped hands.

"Mike," Jamie urged, when it seemed he would not continue, "please finish."

Tension hovered between them, then he complied. "At a celebration following a particularly successful business trip Michelle encouraged him to drink heavily. Then she maneuvered him into a room in the hotel where the meetings were being held and set up a scene for some photographs. They were to be her insurance for further advancement. Instead, it destroyed three people—my father, my mother, and herself."

"Wasn't he proved innocent?"

"After it was too late. He died thinking the world believed he had been unfaithful to the principles he had lived his life by. And in reality that's exactly what the world believed."

"No, don't think like that."

"Why not? It's true. The trial got front-page attention, but his vindication wasn't quite so spectacular. All the notice it received was a small article buried on the back pages."

"Maybe the world in general does remember the ugly part, but those who matter didn't need the proof. If your father was a man of such strong convictions, he had to know he would win. Think of it in that light, Mike," she urged. "Always remember: to those who mattered he never changed."

There was no sound in the room. Time stopped as he lifted his head, his gaze capturing hers. "Thank you, Jamie," he said softly, "for believing."

"I'm sorry for what I said before."

"You didn't know."

"Ignorance is no excuse for cruelty."

"You were no more cruel than I. I've done a lot of thinking, honey. What you said was no worse than what I've been guilty of doing to you. From the first moment I met you, I've run roughshod over all you've created in your life. Your life-style didn't suit me, so I set out to change it. I've tried to tell you how to wear your hair, how to dress, and in the height of my arrogance I've even tried to dictate how you should behave with your family. Even after I found out why you live your life as you do, I tried to change it."

"But you never meant me harm," Jamie interjected.

"I'd never willingly hurt you, Jamie."

"I think, perhaps, you're very much like your father—strong and gentle. You didn't deserve what I said that morning. It was absolute perversity, nothing more."

"Maybe, but I drove you to it."

Jamie laughed. "For the first time tonight we agree. You do drive me to perversity, along with 'to distraction'."

Mike's welcome chuckle joined with her clear, healing laughter. "About the perversity I'm sorry. But I must admit that the thought of driving you to distraction has a certain appeal."

"Oh, you . . . you . . ." She searched helplessly for a suitable word.

"How about sweet, wonderful, irresistible rogue?" he offered hopefully.

"Yes, sweet rogue. Thank you."

"Too bad. Maybe the irresistible part will come later, but you're welcome."

"Welcome to what?" she quipped, feeling richly and unbelievably happy. As the import of her words sank in, she blushed and hid her face in the pillow.

"That's one question I don't think I'll answer just yet. We both need some time. You were right when you said this had all happened too fast."

"What can we do?" Her voice was low, the laughter gone.

"We can start again."

"How can that help?" she asked dubiously.

"We can get to know each other all over again. Start fresh, this time with more understanding."

"I wonder if we can."

"Sure we can. All we have to do is keep it light. We need to spend time in the company of other people. We need to do the sort of things other couples do when they first meet and begin to date. We went from A to Z and skipped a few steps in between."

She laughed. "And whose fault was that?"

"Touché." Mike grinned ruefully. "But from the first moment we met you were running away. I didn't have time for a routine courtship, so I had to resort to desperate measures. This time we'll take it slow and easy. You don't run and I won't rush. I'll be the perfect gentleman."

"You devil! You're going to tease me and you know it." She looked into his laughing eyes. "You're doing it now."

"Starting over doesn't mean we can't have fun. I didn't say I wouldn't tease you. That would take all the fun out of my life. We're going to get to know each other and have fun *while* we're both being gentlemen," he said, tongue in cheek.

"*We're* being gentlemen? You don't think I can be a lady, huh? Well, I'll show you. I'll be the most perfect lady. You can open doors for me, take my arm when I cross the street, carry heavy packages for me, the whole bit. When I get through with you"—she blessed him with a wicked smile—"you'll be exhausted from all the chivalry."

"Is that a challenge?"

"You're darn right it is."

"Then I accept. We'll see who's the most perfect lady or gentleman. How about beginning with dinner tomorrow?"

"I can't." A flicker of some strange emotion dulled her eyes for a fleeting instant, then was gone. "Tomorrow I have to practice with Nicky's Little League team. I promised Simon I'd fill in while he was out of town."

Mike studied the calm expression on her face. He was puzzled by something in her manner. The teasing animation of only seconds ago was gone; in its stead was something he could not interpret. "You don't want to practice with the boys? I thought you liked children."

"I do," she protested. "I do want to help Simon and I love children. It's just that—"

"Just what, Jamie?" She was acutely uncomfortable. Why? Mike wondered.

"Nothing." She shrugged, dismissing his concern. "Tomorrow it's the park for me, but if you have no plans for Friday, we can put our challenge to the test. Mom asked me to invite you to a family picnic."

"Aren't you being a little overconfident? How can you be a lady surrounded by your brothers? I don't think the perfect lady plays touch football or climbs trees."

"Says who?" Jamie demanded, slipping back into

their teasing routine. "Just because I've decided to let you open a few doors for me doesn't mean I've become helpless."

"Sure." He grinned innocently. "If you don't think you can do it, I'll take a forfeit."

"Forfeit, my foot. We don't have a bet, so how can I forfeit? And anyway, who said I had?"

"Ah, Jamie, that was the most beautifully fractured phrase yet." His laugh seemed to reach every quiet corner of the room.

"Fractured phrase or not, this is one time I'm going to get the best of you."

"Think you can manage it, what with the football and all?"

"Of course, I can, and anyway, Mom said the rule for this picnic was absolutely and positively *no* football." She grinned at him in happy triumph.

"I think I've been had."

"Would you like to back out?" she asked in mock concern.

"Not on your life. The stakes are too high. I have the feeling that the outcome of this experiment might determine the direction of our future."

"As a lady and a gentleman?"

"As lovers."

"Mike, you promised."

"I did, didn't I?"

"You most certainly did, and if this is any example, you might as well concede defeat right now. A gentleman does not, and I repeat, does not speak to a lady about being lovers."

"All right, my lady expert, what else is it a gentleman doesn't do?"

"For one thing a gentleman doesn't hold or kiss or confuse a lady. He never touches her except in an act of chivalry." Jamie delivered the pronouncement in lofty tones, then ruined the effect by dissolving into a fit of giggles at Mike's look of dismay.

"Jamie." He faced her and spoke with utter, quiet sincerity. "This isn't Friday, and I've missed you."

For a timeless second her heart leaped crazily in her breast. Then a flick of her wrist sent the pillow flying and with laughter bubbling in her throat, Jamie went into his waiting arms.

The sounds of summer filled the park. An early-evening breeze played among the tall pines as they swayed with a soft murmur. Battered swings creaked gently in the dappled sunlight. For a moment a dust devil swirled and twisted, tossing about an abandoned candy wrapper, while the putter of a distant lawn mower faded with a sigh. The crack of a bat, the slap of pigskin against leather, the laughter of a child, blended together in peaceful harmony.

"Alll riiight!" It was a soft, drawling command. "Let's talk it up out there. Let's have a little chatter." Instantly young voices rose to chorus, in an endless chant, the lingo of the game.

They were an unremarkable group of kids, dressed in their scruffiest clothes. But to the man leaning on the chain-link fence, one figure stood apart; smaller than most, shapelier, and with a single braid swinging over her shoulder.

She wore grubby jeans and tennis shoes even more tattered than before. Emblazoned on the front of her orange T-shirt, which was three sizes too large, were two crossed bats and the legend SUPERCOACH. Across the back was simply her name, the *i* dotted with a star.

Even with her shirt hanging nearly to her knees and a baseball cap cocked rakishly over one eye, she was breathtaking to Mike, who had moved heaven and earth to be here. After a restless day of growing concern, he had heedlessly and even foolishly shifted schedules, neglected calls, and canceled meetings. He drove his hapless secretary to distraction in his grim determination to find the cause of the swiftly hidden wariness that had dulled Jamie's eyes at the mention of today's practice.

He watched her as she kicked the dust from home plate, then, calling out names, pounded ball after ball into the field with an astonishing and rhythmic accuracy. She stopped frequently to correct or to praise, and the boys listened raptly, courteously, obeying instantly.

Pointing to one small boy, Jamie relinquished the bat, jogging rapidly to fill the vacancy. A smile tugged at Mike's lips as she efficiently moved from position to position, demonstrating and instructing, laughing and teasing, always praising, while batter after batter took his turn at the plate. It was clear she had done this before, that she was good at it, that she loved it, and that the boys adored her.

"That's it, boys. No more for today," she called in a lilting voice as she wiped the dust from her face with the sleeve of her shirt.

"Aw, Jamie, can't we play a game? Just a short one? Please?" the young voices pleaded in concert.

"Can't. We don't have enough players."

"Timmy Sawyers is over at the playground, and if you play, that will make us only one short. C'mon, Jamie, please." Nicky wheedled in his best and most persuasive manner.

Jamie stood perfectly still, her face stern. Then with a slight nod, a smile broke over her lips. "You're just a bunch of con men, do you know that?"

"Hooray! Hooray! Choose up. I get Jamie."

"No, you don't!"

"Hey, fellas, if we're going to do this, let's do it right," Jamie interceded. "The co-captains will choose. I'll play for the team that comes up short. Here, we'll flip to see who gets first choice."

"Hi, coach, can I play?" Mike's deep voice cut into the melee of childish chatter.

"Mike!" Jamie whirled from the huddle to face him. "When did you get here?" A blush started at her hair-line and spread over her already flushed face.

"I've been here for a while. Good practice," he drawled as he watched her flush deepen.

"I get Mike," Nicky declared to the other captain. "You can have Jamie."

"Traitor." Jamie slanted a grin and a wink at her nephew. "Going with the big guys, are you?"

"Gee, Jamie." The small boy scuffed a toe in the dirt. "He's so big, I bet he can hit more home runs than even you."

Mike's chuckle drew her eyes to him. Of their own volition they moved over him from head to toe. Unable to ignore the way her heart slammed against her ribs, she absorbed how Mike's sweatshirt with its hacked-off sleeves lovingly and faithfully followed every line of his massive shoulders and chest, and how the jeans, riding low, threatened to give in to gravity. She stifled the urge to touch him and gathered her team about her. She announced, "Well, fellas, it looks like it's Mike's Giants against Jamie's Midgets. May the best team win."

She had thrown down the gauntlet and the boys, both small and tall, were caught in the spirit of competition. They played fast and furiously—hitting, fielding, sliding, always on the move, their laughter infectious. Jamie played a mean shortstop and wielded a wicked bat. Mike ranged center field with his borrowed glove like a centaur. Because of his size he insisted, to Nicky's disgust, that he bat left-handed and hit religiously into a waiting fielder's glove.

It was not long before the boys, with the wisdom of the very young, realized that the real game was not between the teams, but rather between their tiny coach and the gigantic substitute. They watched and listened, hiding grins and giggles behind grubby hands. Mike teased Jamie and she baited the bear.

Mike's bat cracked, and for the first time the ball flew to left field. He moved rapidly around the bases, trying for an extra one when, on a bad hop, the ball eluded the fielder. He stretched his luck too far, though, and Jamie tagged him out at third. He rose from the dirt with a lopsided grin on his face.

"Good play, coach." In a friendly pat, his hand caressed the curve of her hip, enticingly outlined by the snug jeans.

"Stop it!" she yelped.

"Stop what?" A wicked gleam lit his eyes, his expression studiously innocent.

"You know what." Jamie rounded on him, meeting his devilish smile with a straight face.

"Do you mean this?" Before she could move, he had again traced the slight swell of her backside, punctuating it with two swift pats.

"Mike!" Jamie threatened.

"Aw, gee, coach, what's wrong with that?" He winked. "All the guys on television do it."

"This isn't television and I'm not their coach."

"No," he agreed, "but I bet they wish they had one like you—coach."

"Don't call me coach." Jamie stalked away, motioning her team with her. Silently daring them to giggle one more time, she picked up a bat, muttering dire threats.

"Did you say something, coach?" Mike stood at her side, bending to retrieve his glove. Jamie only glared at him and turned away, refusing to rise again to the bait.

The pace of the game escalated. Jamie threw herself into it with a feverish intensity, trying to forget the swift surge of nameless excitement that threatened to swamp her senses at his every touch.

And touch her, he did. A pat on the shoulder, a quick tweak of her braid. Once as he jogged past her on the baseline, he gently flicked a speck of dust from the tip of her nose.

She stepped to the plate, her eyes drawn only to him. He had moved from the outfield and stood grinning confidently at first base, the borrowed glove inadequate protection for his hand. A blade of grass was caught in his hair and Jamie longed to brush it away, an excuse to feel Mike's crisp hair beneath her fingers. She hadn't realized she was staring until a small plaintive voice chastised her for her inattention.

"C'mon, Jamie. This is the last out. We've got a chance to score."

Flustered, she ducked her head, unwilling to meet the knowing look he flashed her. Could he read her thoughts? she wondered. With grim determination she gripped the bat and swung. Too late, the ball veered to the right, dribbling in slow, lazy bounces toward first base. Jamie ran and in one desperate lunge dived headfirst, her hand outstretched for the elusive base and safety.

"Yer out, honey." A deep velvet chuckle flowed over her.

Flat on her stomach at his feet, the dust threatening to choke her, frustration spilled over. Like a miniature Venus rising from a sea of red Georgia dirt, she stood, drawing herself to her most regal posture, oblivious of the grass stains at her knees and the long white smear of chalk dust across her shirt. With her head held high she stepped closer, making a tactical error. Now she had to lean back to look into his grinning face. Refusing to give ground, her hands indignantly on her hips, she flew into battle.

"I was safe."

"Was not."

"Was."

"Not."

"Blast it, man—"

"Ah, ah, ah, honey. Don't forget, little pitchers have big ears. Mustn't swear." His finger wagged beneath her nose.

She slapped it away. "Don't you tell me what to do you big . . . big—"

In a quick swoop his mouth came down on hers, silencing her effectively. It was meant to be only a quick, teasing kiss, but neither had reckoned with the sizzling tension that had been thinly masked by the banter of the game. He didn't touch her, yet she was as captivated as if his massive arms had wound themselves about her. Her lips parted and neither remembered where they were.

"Yuck! Kissing a girl. Phooey."

Sanity returned with embarrassing clarity. Jamie drew back guiltily, but not before she heard him groan. "God, sweetheart, what're you doing to me?"

Refusing to meet his eyes, she turned away, hiding the blush that warmed her face. "Jackie," she called, more to relieve her tension than because it mattered, "quit rolling around in the grass and wipe that silly grin off your face!"

"Tell you what, team." Mike's voice broke into the gale of giggles that followed. "You put away the equipment and I'll spring for Cokes. Deal?"

Over the heads of the enthusiastic boys Jamie smiled her thanks for the diversion, then busied herself supervising the storing of the equipment.

Jamie was alone. She had sent the boys ahead to the picnic tables to wait for Mike and the cold drinks he had promised. She hurried across the deserted ballfield, making a final check of the equipment shed and securing the gates. When she turned to make her way to join the boys, she heard them. The motorcycles.

There were three of them, black, shiny, and heavily chromed. They were not the lightweight machines of the casual riders, but the monstrous cycles of hardcore bikers.

Jamie stopped where she was, waiting quietly, hoping against hope that they wouldn't see her. But luck was not with her. With a flourish and a flurry of dust all three of them drew to a skidding halt, hemming her in against the chain link fence.

"Well, well, well, what have we here?" The taller of the three grinned at her, his cold eyes staring pointedly at her shirt. "SUPERCOACH again."

"Let me pass." She spoke evenly, forcing herself to remain calm and ignore the fright that was twisting through her. She knew instinctively that any show of the fear that was pounding in her brain would be her downfall.

"What's your hurry, doll? We haven't seen you in a while. Don't you want to spend a little time with us? Haven't you missed us?" The shorter blond, with almost colorless eyes, stroked her braid insolently, letting his hand linger at her breast.

"I asked you to let me pass," Jamie repeated, refusing to show her revulsion at the intimate touch.

"Now, baby doll." His voice was a low suggestive croon. "Just you wait while old Whitey here parks his bike and we can have some fun. Right, Frank?" The blond grinned at the man by his side.

The tall biker nodded, pushing down his kickstand

and dismounting in one swift move. He stepped closer to Jamie, laughing when this time she did flinch, though her eyes never wavered.

"Brave little thing, aren't you? But for how long, I wonder? Tell you what. You be nice to us"—his empty eyes seemed to touch and violate every part of her body, and the gripping fear grew within her—"and we'll have no problems. How about you, Rex? You want some of this sweet thing?"

The last remark was directed to the third man, who was still sitting on his bike, leaning indolently against the handlebars. With a shrug and a wave of his tattooed arm he gave them his blessings, electing to remain an amused observer. This frightened Jamie even more as she fought back the shiver that shook her at the sight of the hideously drawn snake that coiled in and out among the letters of his name. And now the fear that clawed at her insides was like a wild animal. Oh, God, Jamie thought. This was worse than the last time. What could she do?

"What's the matter, sugar? Cat got your tongue?" It was Frank who spoke, his big hand gripping her cheeks. Blood filled her mouth as her teeth cut into the tender flesh of her jaw. The pressure increased. "A *quiet*, pretty little thing like you needs a man like me."

"Take your hands off her." The low, soft voice was almost conversational. But only a fool would have missed the thread of steel that ran through it.

"Ah, what have we here?" Whitey whirled to face the newcomer who was even taller than he. "Is this lover boy, sugar? Is he why you avoided us last time? Are you his lady?"

"Yes, she's my lady." Mike's voice was flat, devoid of any emotion. "Now, if your friend wants to keep his arm, he'd better back away."

Mike's full attention was riveted on the three men. Rex was still lounging on his bike, his grin wide and evil. Whitey stood, feet apart, in a challenging stance. Frank grinned through broken teeth, taunting Mike as he silently and cruelly squeezed Jamie's face.

Jamie fought hard to hold them back, but tears filled her eyes, as the excruciating pain radiated through her head. She watched helplessly, afraid for herself, but more afraid for Mike.

"Sorry, fella. She's such a little thing, there's not enough for all of us." Again Frank tightened his grip, drawing a low moan of agony from her.

"Damn you!" In one swift, catlike movement Mike closed the distance between them, all hope of avoiding a confrontation destroyed. Their reflexes were quick, but his were quicker.

The strength of Mike's brutal backhand threatened to tear Whitey's head from his shoulders as it spun him around on his heels and sent him sprawling in the dirt. In a smooth continuation of the same motion, Mike's hand fastened around Frank's throat in a deadly grip. One quick look at his back proved that Whitey was no longer a threat and that Rex remained an observer, his amused smile still firmly in place. Mike's cold glittering gaze swept over them in contemptuous dismissal, then settled with an icy rage on Frank.

"I can kill you where you stand." His grip at Frank's bulging throat tightened painfully. "Or you can let her go—*gently*. The choice is yours."

Stubbornly Frank refused, fumbling at his belt for the chain that hung there.

"That's right, do me a favor. Reach for it. Try it. Give me an excuse. Come on," Mike coaxed, "do it."

For what seemed an eternity Jamie thought he would. Fear for Mike drove all sense of pain from her mind. All she could think was that Frank really would reach for the chain, and that Mike would make good his threat. She could read the cold, savage promise in his eyes.

Suddenly with a feral groan, Frank's fingers relaxed, easing slowly from her aching flesh. His eyes flickered in his face, grown blue from the constricting power of Mike's fingers. His knees began to buckle as he clawed at his throat.

Mike grasped the long, unkempt hair with his free hand and finally lifted his stiff fingers from the grimy throat. He slashed his open hand across Frank's face.

"Mike!" Jamie grabbed at his arm. "Stop! You might kill him." Desperately she dragged at him, trying to stop him. Not for Frank's sake, but for his.

Mike delivered one more blow to the biker, then turned to face any new challengers. There were none. Whitey sat where he had fallen; Rex solemnly shook his head. "Not me, man. I don't want any part of you."

"Then I suggest you and your friends decide to travel."

"Yeah. I do have a sudden hankering to see California." Rex's voice hardened into a vicious command. "Get up, both of you. We've got some riding to do."

He watched as his companions mounted their bikes, then with a small salute, roared away.

Jamie slumped against the fence, her control broken. "Jamie?" Mike's gentle hand at her chin lifted her bruised, battered face. For a timeless moment they stared into each other's eyes, then with a sob Jamie went into his arms.

"Oh, Mike, I was so afraid for you." Her words fell damply into the smooth knit of his shirt as she burrowed deeper into his arms.

"For me! My sweet little fool, don't you realize that if either of us had made the wrong move, he could have snapped your neck like a matchstick? God, honey."

In a torrent of tears Jamie sobbed out disjointed words of her fear. "I remembered what you said about your father. The gentleness, the constant fear of harming someone. I knew . . . I thought . . . I was afraid . . . if you'd killed him, it would've been my fault and you would've hated me for it."

"Shh. Hush, love," He stroked her head, smoothing back the loose tendrils that had escaped her braid. "I really wouldn't have killed him. He was only a stupid kid. Maybe this taught him a lesson. And"—he set her from him so that he could look her squarely in the face, his hands resting lightly on her shoulders—"I hope it taught you a lesson too. This isn't the first time this has happened, is it?"

"No," Jamie whispered, dropping her eyes, unable to meet his accusing look. "But it wasn't so bad the other time."

"But you didn't tell anyone, did you?"

"No. I was—"

"You were afraid that your brothers might get hurt, weren't you?"

Jamie nodded miserably, realizing now how foolhardy she had been. A shudder racked her slender frame at the thought of what would have happened if Mike had not been there.

He gently gathered her back against the solid safety of his chest. "Shh, shh. It's over now. Nobody will ever hurt you again. I promise."

He held her through the storm of tears, waiting patiently for some modicum of her normal control to return. When at long last the sobs dwindled into small hiccuping sighs, he dried her tears, and walked her slowly through the park.

Chapter Nine

"Get some rest, then put on your best bib and tucker, honey. I'll be back at seven. Tonight's a special night. I want you to help me celebrate." He kissed her on the upturned nose, tapped it gently, and turned back to the elevator.

Jamie watched until the doors closed him from sight. Then, quietly bemused, she let herself into her apartment. She walked down the hall, loosening the coil of hair that lay heavily against her neck. With her fingers she combed free the snarls as it tumbled down her back to her waist. In her room, still lost in a very private world, she mechanically went about her nightly routine. Her creamy chiffon blouse was unbuttoned and dropped along with a scrap of a bra onto the floor. Next she slithered the slim skirt over her hips, stepping daintily out of the pool it formed around her ankles.

The half-slip, shoes, and panties followed in rapid succession. Gathering them carelessly, she tossed them onto the bed.

Jamie was tired and confused. The three weeks that had passed since the picnic had been filled with one activity after another. It had been fun, it had been exciting—even exhilarating, and through it all Mike had been the perfect gentleman. Though it was a competition of sorts, it was one most unfamiliar to Jamie. Every minute she spent with Mike she was striving to prove all the things she had denied before. It had been difficult at first, but gradually she had learned to accept and even enjoy his courtesies. She was discovering more and more with each passing day that to be a woman was marvelous.

She walked into the bathroom. Perhaps a shower would shake the cobwebs from her brain. The tiles were cool to her bare feet as she flipped the plug into place and turned the taps, adjusting the temperature. It was only as she was shaking a scented bath oil into the swirling water that she remembered she had meant to take a shower.

"Par for the course," she muttered. "Since that maddening man came into my life, I've been totally brainless. How could anyone with a grain of intelligence reach the ripe old age of twenty-six and be such an idiot? First I wasn't happy when he was pressuring me and now I'm not pleased when he's acting the perfect gentleman. Why in heaven he gives me the time of day is beyond me. I can't even take a shower by myself."

Jamie stepped cautiously into the steaming water.

Remembering that her hair cascaded down her back, she picked up a ribbon from the floor. A quick twist, a tight knot, and the heavy mane was out of the way. She sat down in the fragrant water. In a determined effort she blanked all thought from her mind and waited for the heat to work its magic.

The drone of the running water lulled her into a light sleep. A soft lapping about her breasts awakened her. With an extended leg and an agile toe she turned the taps to stop the flow. Leaning back again, she slipped farther beneath the water, letting its warmth soothe her aching nipples.

Lately, at the most inopportune and disconcerting moments, that particular part of her anatomy had become an annoyance. Before they had responded only to hot or to cold: now they grew turgid and ultrasensitive with only a look or a touch from Mike. How many times had she resisted the urge to cross her arms over her chest? How many times had she seen Mike flick his eyes over her, fully aware of her reaction? How many times had she cursed her penchant for silky, clinging blouses and bras that were hardly there? Rats! She had lost all control over her body as well as her mind.

Tossing aside the soap, Jamie slipped even farther beneath the water. Leaning back, she rinsed away the foamy lather, then employing the agile toes again, she flipped the plug, watching the bubbles as they curled and turned in a downward rush. Ignoring that she was dripping on the floor, she stepped from the tub. Using a bright green towel she rubbed her body vigorously.

"Now." She walked into her bedroom and stood

before her open closet, "What do I have to wear for a special occasion?"

Her wardrobe was adequate, but not large. She was inclined to hang on to comfortable old favorites rather than keep up with the current trends. Critically she surveyed her choices. As she looked through her closet, memories of past weeks filled her mind.

The teal-blue T-shirt had been worn to the family picnic. Even now she could feel the heat of Mike's eyes as she had cuddled Seth and Jenny's newborn child to her breast. His look had held a caress, but she could not quite read the carefully expressionless face he presented. She had no idea what he was thinking, but her close-fitting shirt had left little doubt of her response to his intensity.

The flaming red dress she had worn the only time Mike had taken her dancing. True to his word that they should spend time with other people, he had invited Meg and Andrew along. They had proved a congenial foursome. Andrew and Mike shared a gleeful fondness for teasing, and Meg, for all her worldliness, proved to be as gullible as Jamie. Throughout the evening Mike had played his role to perfection. Even on the dance floor he held her circumspectly. While Jamie fought the urge to burrow herself in his arms and rest her head against his chest, he showed no desire to draw her close. Before the evening was over, under a false gaiety, Jamie harbored a curious resentment.

The thick yellow terry robe that she wore when she washed her hair had given him pause. Arriving two hours earlier than expected one evening he had found her dressed just so, preparing to battle her dripping, tangled hair. Taking the brush and comb from her hands, he had sat behind her and slowly and tenderly smoothed away each snarl. Long after there was need, he had brushed the shimmering tresses. Then, after burying his face in the fragrant silk, he had stood, smiled, and left her to dress.

The white tennis dress drew a chuckle from Jamie. Gleefully she recalled how Mike had agreed to drive with her in her car to a tennis match. She had stood on the curb, racket in hand while he bent, folded, spindled, and mutilated himself to get his long frame into the VW. Jamie had very carefully neglected to tell him her seats were frozen permanently in the first position. Despite all her efforts to the contrary, she could not smother her giggle.

Mike had very solemnly regarded his knees doubled near his chin and the racket wedged between his feet. Then with a look that spoke volumes as he surveyed her own body, he said, "Limitations, honey."

She had worn the mauve sundress the night they had argued. Mike had taken her to a delicatessen in a large hotel. In their continuing contest in manners and graciousness he had insisted that she should precede him into the revolving door. Jamie was just as adamant that he should go first and help her with the leaving of it. Mike had, outrageously, taken it upon himself to conduct a poll right there on the sidewalk. An elderly lady with a twinkle in her eyes suggested that the best way for a handsome young man to escort his lovely date through was by her side. Then, if perchance the door should stop, the handsome young man should follow his own instincts. Mike found the idea delightful.

With gallant grace he led Jamie into the slowly moving cubicle. She never knew how he did it, or if by some remote chance it was coincidence, but the door did stop and Mike did follow his instincts.

For the first time in days Jamie had felt the warmth of his arms about her. His lips had brushed across hers in a light kiss, then returned for more as her arms slid about his waist. Deeper and deeper into his embrace she sank as time stopped. It was only the imperious pounding in her ears that drew her back to reality. Her face still burned with a blush as she remembered the smiling faces of the people crowded around, waiting to pass through the door. She had become more chagrined when she saw that it had not been knocking she heard, but the applause of their captive audience. With her face hidden against his chest, she let Mike lead her from the door. She had heard only dimly the pleasant remarks of encouragement the grinning males in the group offered. Mike had just tightened his arms about her and murmured his thanks to the gleeful compliments.

The food of the well-known and popular sandwich shop might have been cardboard. Jamie had no taste for it, while Mike calmly ate enough for an army. The unsettling time in their glass cage had obviously been banished from his mind. And, not for the first time, Jamie both envied and resented his iron control.

"Iron control?" she muttered, bringing herself back from her memories. "We'll just see." Swiftly brushing aside her old standbys, she dug deep into the back of her closet. There, hanging by her favorite sweatshirt, was her one and only Paris creation. It was black lace, what there was of it. From a halter top it plunged to the waist in front, and there was no back. Jamie had never worn it; indeed, hadn't even bought it. It had been a gift from her roommate at St. Anne's.

Catherine had a Frenchwoman's weakness for clothes, often buying on impulse. On a visit to her family she had seen this dress and bought it, never considering that black was not her color. After wearing it once, she had tossed it to Jamie, declaring, "On you it will be stunning. In it I become a corpse."

Jamie had laughed at her dramatics and accepted the dress, knowing she would never wear it. At least she had never thought she would.

Quickly, before she could lose her courage, she selected what little lingerie the dress would allow. A bra was definitely out. A wicked gleam lit her face when she anticipated Mike's reaction. He'd probably wait all evening for her to shrug.

"Ha! You'll have a long wait, Mr. Bradford."

Dressing with particular care, she eyed herself critically at every turn. Leaving her hair down, she wove a silver ribbon in and around its strands, giving the effect of a loose, heavy braid. On impulse she fastened a long, delicate chain about her neck, from which dangled a tiny silver heart that nestled between her breasts. After a final application of mascara, she stepped back to survey her handiwork.

"Shoes!" she exclaimed. "Jamie, you need shoes." Scrabbling again into the far reaches of her closet, she drew out a pair of black sandals with shockingly high heels. Slipping into them, she turned again to the mirror. Inordinately pleased with the total effect, she giggled, pirouetting ungracefully on the unfamiliar heels. This brought on a new spate of giggles. When she had regained a measure of control, she looked down at her feet ruefully.

"False courage maybe, but I need every inch I can get." The doorbell chimed. "The marines have landed, Jamie. It's too late to retreat. Remember, walk carefully, Short Stuff, and whatever you do, stand straight."

The bell rang three more times in rapid succession. "I'm coming, I'm coming." She walked cautiously, wobbling only a bit. She threw the door open grandly and waited for Mike's astonishment.

"Hi." He stepped past her, brushing a kiss across her ear. His arms were filled to overflowing with gaudy packages. "By the way," he tossed over his shoulder, "I like your shoes."

"My shoes?"

"Sure, but I hope you don't fall off them and break your pretty little neck."

"I stand here looking like a French floozy and he likes my *shoes*?" she muttered. "Well." She forgot and shrugged. "Chalk one up to the femme fatale."

"Did you say something, love?" Mike dumped the packages onto the sofa and turned to her. "Happy birthday."

"It's not my birthday."

"I know, it's mine."

"It's your birthday and you brought your own presents?"

"They're yours."

"We've already established it's your birthday, not mine."

"Patience, honey, I'll explain."

"Do you think you can?" she drawled.

"Sure. Come sit by me and open your packages while I tell you."

"You can tell me anything you want, but I can't take those presents."

"Why not?" Mike asked reasonably.

"Because . . . because . . ." She could think of no sensible answer.

"Hush your stuttering, honey, and come listen to me." He took her hand, drawing her down beside him. "When I was a kid, my mother thought I was a trifle selfish. I had more than I could ever play with, but I stubbornly refused to share. So she started the practice of giving gifts on our birthdays, rather than receiving. I learned there is an immeasurable pleasure in giving. So"—he paused and grinned engagingly—"surely you aren't going to spoil my birthday by refusing my presents."

"You idiot." Jamie laughed. "What woman could refuse you when you ply your charms?"

"That, my love, is about the most ungraceful acceptance I've ever heard. Here, open this one first."

"I really shouldn't." She looked at him solemnly for a second, then broke into a grin. "What the heck, it's your birthday." Rapidly she disposed of ribbon and paper. A pale blue box was revealed. Inside was a small gold bracelet with one charm.

"A garbage can?"

He nodded. "To commemorate our meeting. Here, let me put it on you."

Jamie watched as his fingers fumbled with the tiny

catch. Holding the bracelet to the light to admire its rich gleam, she laughed. "I must be the only woman in the city who wears a garbage can around her arm. *Très chic.*"

"On you it is." He kissed the soft skin of her inner wrist. "Now this one."

She took the heavy box from his hand. Dispatching with the wrappings efficiently, she drew out a beautiful round golden ball. "How lovely. What is this on top?"

"It's lapis lazuli—from Afganistan."

"It's the most beautiful paperweight I've ever seen. I'll use it to hold only my most important papers," she teased. "Look! The stone changes color. It was blue and now it's almost violet."

"Like your eyes," he murmured.

"My eyes are blue, not violet," she contradicted.

"There are times, Jamie, when your eyes are deeply violet."

"When?"

"I'll show you sometime, I promise. Next."

With a soft laugh Jamie slipped the ribbon free. "Oh, my. A butterfly." Gently, she lifted it from the nest of protective tissue. A tiny yellow butterfly perched on a round porcelain box that was banded by antique silver. It opened when Jamie pressed the catch, revealing a key. "I've never seen anything so breathtaking. Is there a name for it?"

"The box is a *tabatière*, an eighteenth-century snuffbox, to be exact."

"I've heard of those. I can't take it, it's too valu-

able. There are collectors all over the world looking for
these." She tried to push the delicate box into his hand.

"No, Jamie. The box is yours. It has no great value, except to us. I chose it because the butterfly is like
you. Beautiful, graceful, and,"——he laughed——"hard to
catch. Keep it. I knew it was meant for you the minute
I saw it."

"I don't know what to say."

"Don't say anything yet. There's more to come.
This one's next."

"Wait a minute," Jamie said. "You didn't tell me
what the key is for."

"That's a special surprise for later. I'll keep it for
you if you'd like."

"You do love a good mystery, don't you?" She
smiled fondly as he pocketed the key. Then she turned
her attention to the package resting in her lap. "This is
a weird one."

"Not so weird. Open it."

"You devil! No fair. I'm supposed to be a lady,
which, according to your dictates, means no football.
And then you give me a football."

"It's something every lady quarterback should
have."

"Does this mean the challenge is over?"

"Not on your life, madam."

"Then you're using dirty tactics. How can any red-
blooded athlete resist trying out a new ball?"

"Maybe this will distract you for a while." He passed a bulky square box to her.

"A chocolate kiss that weighs ten pounds."

"But not as good as the real thing. Next."

"*The Layman's Guide to the Rules of Touch Football.*"

"In case you forget how to play."

"A teddy! Do women really wear these things?"

"For a while."

"Mike, I really don't think this is what your mother had in mind when she taught you the pleasures of generosity. I doubt she meant for you to shower quite so much on one person. This is foolish."

"Don't let it worry you, honey. Anyway, there's only one left." In the midst of their playfulness he had become strangely serious. He lifted the last package from the debris scattered on the floor. "This is the one I'm wondering if you will really like."

"Of course, I will." She tore the wrappings away from the last surprise. "You seem to know instinctively what I—" Her voice failed as the paper fell away.

Mike waited as Jamie stared at his gift. Slowly she lifted it from the box and held it before her. Her hands were shaking.

"If you hate it, Jamie, you could always use it for a dartboard."

"I don't hate it," she murmured.

"Then you like it?"

"Yes. Yes, I like it very much."

"It was a bit vain of me," he admitted with a grin, "but I wanted you to have something to remember me by."

"Remember you by?"

"Yeah. For those long lonely hours when I can't be with you. I want to be sure I stay in your mind."

"I don't need any reminders, but I'll keep this on

my bedside table." Jamie lowered her eyes so Mike could not see the quick shine of tears this special gift had brought. She missed the tender look that crossed his face at her first admission that he was in her thoughts as she was in his.

"Let's leave this," he said huskily, indicating the clutter of papers and ribbons that were scattered over the floor. "There's something else I'd like to show you."

"Let me put this in my room, then I'll be ready to go." Jamie rose to her feet and walked to her room. On the table by her bed, she set the framed likeness of Mike. Because her knees had begun to shake, she sat on the edge of the bed as she stared at the laughing green-eyed man in the photograph.

"Jamie?"

"Coming. Coming right now. Give me a second to check my makeup." She didn't move. Something about his generosity bothered her.

There was an elusive memory darting just beyond her reach. When she thought she had it, it skittered away. What was it? Fiercely she concentrated, groping in the darkest part of her mind.

She remembered! Mike's birthday wasn't until next month. Meg had casually mentioned it in one of their earlier conversations. What was the purpose of tonight? What zany scheme was this, and what crazy surprises were next?

"Jamie." Mike stood in the door. "We'd better get a move on, we've lots to do yet."

"And it's your birthday," she said brightly, allowing herself the pleasure of looking at him as he stood darkly handsome in the pale wash of the lamplight. She had always thought him attractive, but now with his face filled with the joy of giving, he was absolutely breathtaking. He was a kind and generous man, and the love of such a man would be the gift of a lifetime. "It's your birthday," she repeated, "and a very special night."

"A special night," he agreed, his gaze traveling slowly over her face. "Let's make the most of it."

"I intend to," she whispered.

Jamie leaned back into the soft leather comfort of the Corvette. With her head back and her eyes closed she let the sleek sounds of the powerful engine lull her into sleepy tranquility. The gentle vibrations, the slight sway of stops and turns, and the heady scent of his cologne created a cocoon of peace. He muttered once, an unkind description of another's expertise at the wheel. Jamie listened and smiled. It was all a part of this enchanted evening.

"Asleep, my love?" His breath was warm on her cheek and she realized the car had stopped.

"Hmm." She turned her head to face him, her eyes open. "No, not sleeping, only feeling."

"Feeling?"

"Yes, the magic of a beautiful evening. Did I wish you a happy birthday?"

"If you did, I wouldn't mind hearing it again, especially if it's given with a kiss."

Jamie lifted her eyes slowly to meet and hold his. Her hand circled his neck to draw his mouth to hers. Once lightly, then again, she nibbled gently at his lips. In a husky voice she whispered, "Happy birthday, Mike."

It was simply his name, but it could have been a word of love. With all the tenderness of an endearment she murmured his name again and her lips touched his cheek.

"Oh, honey." He gave a shaky laugh. "I think maybe that's all the birthday wishes I can stand for now." He drew in a deep breath as he stroked her cheek. "Come on. There's something I want to show you."

He was out of the car in one smooth, rapid motion and, for the first time, Jamie realized they were not at a restaurant or the park. They were parked in the wide concrete drive of a graceful cedar-and-stone house.

"How beautiful," she exclaimed as she accepted his help from her seat. "Who does it belong to? Are we visiting someone?"

"No. No one else is here." He drew a key from his pocket and unlocked the massive carved door. "It belongs to a very special friend. It's still in the planning stages, but I wanted you to see it."

Jamie's heels echoed in the empty silence of a family room of gigantic proportions. Although there was little furniture and no personal touches, it held a warmth rare in an unoccupied house. Someone had, with loving care, planned and designed a sanctuary.

Silently, offering no comment, Mike led her from one room to another. A country kitchen that promised leisurely family meals; a study, where the man of the house could work or meditate; a game room that needed only children to fill it; a formal dining room for special occasions; four bedrooms that were all empty, except the master suite, which held the largest bed Jamie had ever seen.

Just as silently Jamie followed where he led. They had returned to the family room before Mike spoke. "What do you think of it?"

"It's too much for words. Your friend is a lucky person to have such a place to call home."

Mike watched her intently. For a moment she thought he would speak, but after a slight hesitation, he seemed to change his mind.

"Do I know your friend?" Jamie waited almost in fear of the answer.

Again he seemed about to speak, hesitated, then spoke, leaving her question unanswered. "There's a pool out back. Would you like to see it?"

"Of course. I want the full fifty-cent tour, no short-cuts." Her laugh was brittle, only a caricature of the real thing.

In his eagerness Mike missed the slight trembling of her lips. Taking her hand in his, he led her through the door out onto a terrace that bordered a pool. The water was glistening in the bright light of the setting sun.

"Do you like it?" he asked as he had done before. Jamie was surprised at how anxious he seemed for her approval.

"How could anyone not like this? It looks more like a natural pond one might find in a wooden glen. Mike! It looks like the lake in the park."

"You noticed." He smiled a sleek, satisfied smile

that lit his green eyes with mischief. "Would you like to go for a swim?"

"It would be heavenly, but I'm not into skinny-dipping."

"No problem. Another of your presents, my lady." From his hip pocket he produced a small, flat, tissue-wrapped package. "This should be your size."

Puzzled, Jamie took it from him and stripped the tissue away. "A bathing suit. Or almost one."

"I told you it would look good on you the day we saw it in the window display."

"And I told you I'd get arrested in it." She dangled the skimpy red suit from her fingers.

"Jamie, there's not a cop in sight."

"That's what I'm afraid of." She laughed again in spite of herself.

"Stop arguing, woman, and put it on." His hands at her shoulders urged her toward the cabana at the far side of the pool. "It's hot. A swim is exactly what we need."

She took one tentative step, then turned back to him. "But what about you? Will you swim?"

"Don't look so worried, honey. No skinny-dipping for me either. I have a suit here. Now, scoot." He swatted her smartly on her backside.

"Bully," she retorted, but did as he asked.

When she returned to poolside, he was waiting, bronzed and handsome in deep blue trunks, a heavy towel across his shoulders. As she walked toward him, she could feel his eyes on every part of her body. She lifted her head bravely to challenge that look as he rose to tower over her.

"I knew that suit was meant for you." His hands circled her waist, drawing her nearer. "Do you know, I forget from one minute to the next how very tiny you are?"

Jamie looked down at her bare feet and grinned ruefully. "Without my heels we look even more like Mutt and Jeff than ever."

"You're the prettiest Mutt in the world, that's for sure."

"Who said I was Mutt? I just happen to be the tall guy in this twosome," she protested. "See?" To prove her point, she delivered one strong push, toppling him into the clear water.

She watched as he sank to the bottom, then rose slowly to the surface. The smooth grace of his powerful strokes fascinated her. The muscles of his arms and shoulders rippled as he cut cleanly through the water. Bemused in her admiration, she realized her peril too late. Mike's hand closed around her ankle, and in an instant she splashed, with little elegance, into the pool.

Prepared for battle, she broke the surface only to find herself captured within his firm grasp. "Before you declare war, honey, I think I'd better remind you that what you just did was not exactly ladylike, and I claim a forfeit."

"You think so, huh?" Jamie laughed. "Then you'll have to catch me first." With a splash and a wriggle she was out of his grasp.

Mike was an excellent swimmer, but Jamie was better. Her small body moved agilely with the training of a lifetime. She slithered and turned through the water, always only a fingertip away from his seeking hands. In an aquatic ballet they glided, roving every inch of the pool—first on the surface, then beneath—in a silent chase. Jamie darted like a mermaid, teasing, taunting, almost, but never quite, within his reach. As his big body proved less mobile she grew bolder, drawing nearer and nearer, only to slip away at the last possible second. In her delight in the game she finally miscalculated. As she was rising from the bottom at the shallow end with her hair swirling down, Mike's hands fastened on the silver ribbon in her hair. In one swift swoop he caught her to him, his hands sliding to her waist as he lifted her from her feet.

Having captured his prize, he gripped her tightly, swinging her high into the air so that her thighs pressed against his chest in a cascade of water. Frozen in a breathless tableau, in a shattering millisecond of timeless awareness, both realized Jamie's breasts were bare. With the ribbons of her hair, he had grasped the single tie that held the small triangles in place. Neither stirred. Jamie made no move to cover herself, nor Mike to release her. The heavy breathing of their exertions slowed, halted.

The setting sun sliding behind the gathering clouds bathed sky and water in a fiery hue. In a silhouette against the everchanging light, they stood, his hands about her body, hers resting at his shoulders.

A single drop of water trembled on a lash as she gazed like a frightened gazelle into his eyes. Mesmerized, Mike watched, as in slow motion, like a rivulet of liquid diamond, it trickled down her cheek, her neck, to the soft swell of her breast. On the tip of a dusky nipple it poised, shimmering in the reflected light.

In painful fascination, sliding her body down his, he leaned forward to catch the waiting droplet with his tongue. Beneath the velvet roughness of his caress Jamie's breath quickened and her nipples tautened, darkening in their desire.

"Oh, God." Mike groaned as he took her aching loveliness into his mouth.

Jamie stirred beneath his soothing caress, her breath stopping in her chest. Her hands buried themselves in the sleek wetness of his hair as she pressed his head closer, needing more of him.

"Jamie, honey, I need you. I need you," he muttered almost harshly against her cooling skin. In a graceful move he lifted her from the pool, her body cradled to his.

She never remembered the towel he wrapped so regretfully about her, nor their journey, amid scattered kisses and murmurs, to the master suite. She never remembered his tenderness, nor his sound of sweet pleasure when he removed the last of the tiny bikini from her.

But she would remember for always the beauty of his body as he flung aside his own swimsuit. She would remember for always how, with tantalizing slowness, he lowered her to the welcoming coverlet, touching, stroking, caressing her hungrily. She would remember for always how his body seemed to burn into hers as he took her to the realms of love she had never guessed existed. She would remember for always his exultant cry silenced by her kiss as the world broke into a kaleidoscope of silent, wondrous rapture. She would remember.

• • •

From the depths of a deep and restful sleep Jamie woke with a start, a small cry on her lips. The slow rise and fall of Mike's chest indicated he had not heard.

"What have I done? What madness is this?" Slowly, moving only a bit at a time, she slipped from the bed. Once he stirred and she froze in the darkness, forcing herself to wait as his movements subsided and he returned to the peacefulness of deep sleep. She wanted to run, to leave behind this room, this time, this man who had so completely taken over her mind, her body, and tonight her very soul. She was frightened, for she had given her whole self into the keeping of this man. She had given him the part of her that had always been her salvation. The part that was hers alone. She was frightened as she had never been before.

I have to get away, she thought. *I must!* She searched the room for her clothing, remembering belatedly that it was still in the cabana. What could she do? Wildly her eyes roved the room, seeking a covering for her fear. The towel! It would serve.

"Jamie." A warm, rough hand slid about her waist from behind. The slight roughness of his beard scratched her neck as he kissed her shoulder. "Are you all right?"

"Of course."

He kissed the tip of her ear, whispering, "Darling, I love you." His caressing hand slipped to cup her tender breast, his fingers tangling in the chain of the locket that still rested in the shadowed cleft. "Only one more thing and this will be the most perfect night of my life."

Her cry and her stiffening body startled him. The delicate chain broke and fell unheeded to the floor.

"Honey?" He turned her to face him. "What is it? What's wrong?"

Keeping her head bowed, her eyes down, she refused to answer. Even when he tried to lift her chin, she resisted, jerking away. In a terrified cry, she blurted, "Stop it!"

"Stop?" He looked down at her in bewilderment.

"Yes. Leave me alone. Don't touch me!" She moved farther away from him.

"Jamie, what is it? Tell me." He stared at her searchingly, misunderstanding the stricken look in her eyes. "Oh, damn me for a fool, I hurt you. I should have been—"

"Gentler?" she asked, the bitterness of her fear and self-recrimination heavy in her voice. "Don't worry yourself about it. For a new lover you were perfect. A woman couldn't ask for one more gentle."

"New lover?" He was strangely still.

"That's what you've become tonight, isn't it?" she whispered, refusing to meet his eyes. "It was what you wanted."

"But it's not enough, Jamie. You know that between us it could never be enough." His stare pierced the last of her defenses, and Jamie began to tremble. Unshed tears shone in her eyes. He reached for her then, wanting to hold and comfort her, to wipe the lines of strain from her face. Her muffled sob was an agony to him. "Honey, don't."

"Don't touch me. Please don't. I can't stand anymore."

He stepped back, dropping his arms to his side. The look of hurt and pain that crossed his face rivaled

Jamie's. His voice was barely audible when he spoke. "I said that I love you."

"I know you did, and here in your special friend's house, while you wear the ring of another special friend, I've let myself fall under your spell. I thought I could give you what you wanted, be the kind of woman you wanted me to be, but I can't. I can't! I've been an awful fool."

He shook his head as though trying to clear it. "It would seem that one of us is indeed a fool. But it isn't you, Jamie."

He turned away, standing with his eyes lowered. Then in a jerky motion, he scooped the towel from the floor where he had tossed it another lifetime ago. Securing it with a tuck about his lean waist, he walked to the open door.

"I'll bring your clothes from the cabana. When you're dressed, I'll take you home."

Chapter Ten

The trip back to Jamie's apartment was interminable. Mike was silent graciousness itself, never touching, never speaking. Only the stark white of his knuckles as he gripped the steering wheel gave the lie to his outward calm. Jamie clutched her sides, curled into a ball of living misery.

At the curb before her building she turned to leave the car. His hand at her arm stopped her. "I'll see you to your door."

"It isn't necessary," she whispered.

"It's three o'clock in the morning, Jamie. It's necessary."

How different this ride in the elevator was from the first one they had shared. How unlike that teasing, laughing man he was. His eyes that had flashed with a warm emerald fire were cold and hard. The lips that had curled in a friendly smile were grim. For a man who had only tonight celebrated a premature thirty-third birthday, he seemed older and infinitely tired.

At her door Jamie turned to him, speaking in stilted tones. "Thank you for escorting me. I'll be fine now."

"Not yet, Jamie. We have a bit more to say to each other." He gripped her arm firmly, leading her into the darkness of her apartment. Flipping on the lights as he went, he seated her on the sofa, then stood looking down at her. Jamie waited silently, frightened not of the man, but of what he might say.

His eyes were still glittering with that same cold light as he regarded her slowly. With a gesture of impatient resignation he began to speak. "No matter what you choose to think, I didn't plan this. There are certain—precautions that, in the heat of the moment, neither of us considered. Had I been thinking clearly, I would never have—" He stopped, grimaced ruefully, seemed almost to tremble, then continued. "But then, had I been thinking clearly, tonight would never have happened."

Jamie twisted her hands into a painful knot. She swallowed convulsively, wanting to speak, but the words would not come.

"It would seem that despite our efforts, neither of us truly knows the other. No matter how I tried, I couldn't get you to trust in me, believe in me, and I—" He faltered, his voice quavering for an instant. "Jamie, from the first moment I saw you, I knew I had to have you. You were the woman I had despaired of ever finding. A woman of spirit and courage, one who could be friend as well as lover. I would've asked much of you, Jamie, but given more. If only——" With an abrupt shake of his head he straightened, squaring his shoulders.

Jamie's heart was pounding in her chest. The very force of it took her breath away, threatening to suffocate her. In silence she watched and listened, knowing she had indeed been a fool. A terrible fool.

"Before I leave, I'd like to give you what is yours, has always been yours from the first day I met you." From his finger he drew the sapphire ring. "I bought this that very day. I've worn it constantly, for in it I could see the loveliness of your eyes." He laid it on the table by her side.

"And this"—he set the small key from the snuffbox beside the ring—"is the key to the house. It's yours, Jamie, but I'd hoped you'd let me share it with you as your friend and your lover. The one thing needed to make this the perfect night was a single word."

"A word?" she murmured, trying desperately to assimilate all he was saying.

"Is it so hard to guess the word, Jamie? A simple yes, and we could have shared all our tomorrows, had that beautiful daughter for me to guide, and sons for you to teach."

"Oh, no." Total realization of exactly what she had thrown away ripped through her.

"Maybe, if tonight had never happened, we might at least have remained friends. Still, if ever you need me . . ." He ran his hand over his blank face, his empty eyes never wavering, then with head bowed he walked to the door. He paused there, speaking without turning to her. "Perhaps I'll love again. I hope I do, but it could never be as I would've loved the woman you might have been. You don't really believe all the things you've said to me tonight. You feel threatened by all that I want. First you sent David away, and now me. Someday I hope you will meet a man who can conquer your fears, and when you do, I wish you happiness. Good-bye, Jamie."

Jamie stared at the closed door, ashen-faced, sickness gathering in her. What had she done? Rising as in a trance, she walked to the window overlooking the street. It was as empty as the aching void in her heart. Then Mike stepped into view. She watched as he walked, head down, past his car. He was a shadowy figure in a rising mist of the predawn of the summer morning.

The wisp of fog thickened, clinging to her window, blocking out the street below, fleetingly mirroring her own image. In the harsh, eerie reflection lay the promise of the loneliness of a loveless life. From the darkness rose the specter of Aunt Prue. "Oh, dear God, no."

Weaving its way through the morning, the fog moved on, leaving the street clear and bright. Mike was not there. She stared down into the waning darkness. From the past, fragments of her memory assaulted her with the cold glitter of eyes that looked as if they had forgotten how to smile. She knew she would never escape them, nor the truth he had made her face.

"What is the truth, Jamie?" Like the mist that had hidden then revealed, she forced herself to search the deepest recesses of her heart and mind. Heavy lids drooped, thick lashes lay like spikes of black velvet against her cheeks. Her lower lip trembled until she caught it between her teeth. The very air in the apartment seemed thick and expectant as she slumped against the windowsill. A deep, shuddering breath broke the statuelike stillness of her small body. A frail voice broke the quiet. "I am afraid."

In an instant of blinding clarity Jamie understood herself. She knew that even as she had drawn David to her, she had rejected the total giving his loving had asked. And she had sent him away. Then there was Mike who did not ask, but demanded. In her heart she carried the image of a forgotten smile. He had said she had a power she did not understand and did not use. But she had. She had used it to destroy that smile. Power to destroy? Power to restore? Could she give him back his smile? she asked herself. Did she want to? Yes! Could she? She could try. She desperately wanted to see laughing green eyes lit with the look meant only for her.

Not bothering to change into more suitable clothing, Jamie raced from her apartment, down the walk in the direction he had taken. Calling his name over and over again, she ran until she was exhausted. He was nowhere in sight, but he couldn't be far. Where could he have gone? She thought frantically. The park! He would go to the park, and to the island.

Mindless of the stitch in her side, she began to run again. This time she ran silently, conserving her strength, not wasting her precious breath calling his name. She ran for six blocks until she was stopped by the gate at the entrance. Locked! She shook it hard and it opened with a soft squeak. Thank God. And again she ran, down the walkways and public paths and onto the wooded trails.

Even in the heat of the summer night the woods were dank and cool. There had been a light playful breeze at first, but now it had grown fierce and angry. Low-hanging limbs tore at her hair, briars imbedded themselves in her soft flesh. Once a stone rolled beneath her feet, causing her ankle to turn painfully. She ignored it. She ignored everything except her goal.

Loose strands of her hair were tossed about her face. Impatiently she slashed a dark curl from her eyes as she broke into the clearing. She paused there at the forest's edge, all sounds muffled in the oppressive air. Only the steady drip of a few remaining raindrops left by a prestorm shower broke the stillness. Below her, strangely calm in the brewing storm, was the little island surrounded and protected by the jeweled waters of the lake. Like a castle and its moat, Jamie thought, safe from the vagaries of the world.

Thunder rumbled deep and fierce in the distance. Lightning split the sky, filling the clearing with the brightness of midday. Fleeting as it was, it was enough to imprint the changes on her mind. Long after the light had faded, she saw the sparkle of the water, the golden glow of a multitude of marigolds planted with a loving hand. In her mind's eye she could see the carefully trimmed walk, the graceful arch of the footbridge, strong and safe. And the gazebo restored. His gift to her. An expression of the love that had been thrown back into his face by a foolish, stupid girl who had been afraid to be a woman.

Thunder sounded again, nearer now. On its heels

came a jagged flash of lightning. She didn't need this second revelation to know the clearing was deserted. He wasn't there.

The first cold drops of rain fell, mingling with the tears that streamed down her cheeks. She began to stumble down the hillside toward the lake. Slowly at first, then she began to run. Down and across the meadow, over the bridge to the island. She paused before the gazebo. In the rain the marigolds bowed their heads and water poured off the roof of the ancient structure, but the newly constructed floor and benches, dry and protected, beckoned her inside.

For her. No one had to tell her. He had done it for her. Slowly she mounted the steps, running her hands caressingly over the smooth, beautiful railing. Forgetting that her soaked clothing might mar the polished floor, she sat staring bleakly at the rain, wondering what she would do with the rest of her life.

"He's back!" Meg stood in Jamie's doorway.

Jamie looked up from the translation she had just begun. "Who's back?"

"Jamie," Meg said gently, "this is Meg, remember? You don't have to pretend with me."

Pain flitted across Jamie's carefully composed features. For only a moment she allowed herself to yield to the ache that had never left her. Six weeks of fighting the black depression had gained her no ground. Would it fade soon? Or was she destined to walk the earth as an imitation of a real, living human being? For these long, empty weeks, she had existed, nothing more.

"Jamie, are you okay?"

"Yes, Meg." Jamie gathered her courage about her. "I'm fine." Nervously she moistened her lips. In a low voice she asked, "Have you seen him?"

"No, but the grapevine says he looks awful."

"Has he been ill?" Jamie was alarmed.

"I doubt it." Meg eyed her friend, thinking she looked like the one who had been ill. "It's probably more a case of driving himself to forget a broken heart."

"Don't, Meg. Please don't."

"All right, Jamie." There were tears of compassion in Meg's eyes. "I won't say anymore, but I do think you're making a mistake. See him. Tell him how you feel. The man cares for you, I know he does. A man like Mike doesn't give his love casually to be turned off and on like a light. See him."

"I can't," Jamie insisted stubbornly. "If he had ever wanted to see me again, he wouldn't have vanished the next day without so much as a word. I tried for a week to reach him. You know I couldn't."

"He didn't vanish, for goodness' sake! He went on a business trip. He used to do it all the time."

"Perhaps he did, but he left no messages for me then because he didn't want to see me, and I have no reason to think he might have changed."

Meg studied her friend for the space of a thought, then decided to take matters into her own hands. "I guess you're right. What you need now is to get the man completely off your mind. Let's play truant and skip out early for a long leisurely lunch. My treat."

Jamie demurred. "Thanks, but I have work to do."

"How much work do you expect to get done sitting there thinking about Mike?"

"Probably none," Jamie answered honestly.

"So! I have the perfect solution. We'll go out to lunch, drink a scandalously expensive bottle of wine, or even two, and forget our troubles. How about it? Are you game?"

"Our troubles? Meg, are you and Andrew having problems?"

"Didn't he tell you?"

"No. He hasn't said a thing."

Meg crossed her fingers behind her back, composed her face into a convincing mask of hurt and confusion, and invented madly. "We had an awful quarrel last night, Jamie. Maybe if I had someone to talk to, it would help."

"Oh, Meg, you and Andrew are so right for each other, surely you can solve any problems you have."

"I'm not so sure." Meg's red curls bobbed about her sad face.

"If I can help, I will," Jamie said.

"What I need right now is a shoulder to cry on. Come to lunch and I'll cry over my wine."

"All right," Jamie answered solemnly, rising from her seat. "Just give me a minute to freshen up."

In the lounge Jamie surveyed herself in the mirror. She was pounds thinner. Interesting hollows had appeared beneath her cheeks, hollows that worried her mother no end. In a fit of self-hatred she had cut her hair and had indeed changed her appearance. The hair hadn't become the mass of unruly curls she'd feared, but fell in shimmering waves about her shoulders. The sophistication she had always sought was almost hers.

"Ready?" She turned to Meg, who was standing at her side.

"Sure."

"Where are we going?"

"I thought maybe Jean-Charles's."

Jamie did not answer, but silently followed her companion from the lounge. Meg chatted brightly to the morose Jamie all through the short cab ride across town. It was only as they were seated at their table that she fell silent, scanning the tables nearby.

Following the direction of her gaze Jamie gasped, her face livid with horror. At the table by the window Mike was sitting with Lisa Lang. As Jamie watched him hungrily, he saw her. He inclined his head curtly in greeting, a faint smile on his lips. Only Jamie knew it wasn't really a smile. One might think so at first, before seeing his eyes. They were cold and dim, and Mike was a man who smiled with his eyes.

"You knew!" Jamie looked accusingly at Meg.

Before Meg could reply, Jamie rose from her chair, toppling it over. With unseemly haste she rushed through the tables, ignoring the stares of the startled diners. On the sidewalk she frantically summoned a cab. Home, she told herself. She would go home. There she would find some small escape from her pain.

As she was unlocking her door, her telephone was ringing. It would be Meg, she had no doubt. Jamie knew what her friend had tried to do, and she would forgive her. Someday. But not right now; the ache was too new, the pain too raw.

On and on it rang, all afternoon. Finally in a bid for sanity Jamie lifted it off its cradle. Tomorrow would be soon enough to face Meg.

Within the hour her doorbell had taken up where the telephone had ended. On and on it rang insistantly. Obviously Meg had no intentions of giving up. Very well, so be it. Wearily Jamie flung open her door.

It wasn't Meg who stood there, her finger on the bell, but Lisa Lang. Jamie stared into the beautiful face, a face that held no triumph, only pity.

"May I come in?" Lisa asked quietly.

Jamie gestured her in, not trusting herself to speak. Her silence seemed not to bother Lisa in the least. Instead the woman seemed pleased.

"You love him, don't you?" Ignoring Jamie's sudden tensing, Lisa continued. "Don't bother to deny it, it's there in your face."

Jamie dropped her eyes, unable to deny and unwilling to admit. Quiet stretched between them; the ticking of the clock grew thunderous. Then, in defeat, Jamie slumped into a soft cushioned chair. Her voice, raw and ragged, broke the stillness. "Have you come to gloat?"

"No, I've come to tell you what kind of fool you are."

A guttural laugh escaped Jamie's grim lips. "You don't have to tell me. I tell myself with every breath I draw."

"Then perhaps there's hope for you."

"Go away, Lisa. You have him. What more do you want? You've walked away with the prize, I wish you joy." The dark tousled head lifted, the tortured eyes spoke the truth. "Make him happy. He's all you wanted. Handsome and wealthy, and he'll be good to you. But please make him happy."

"You don't know me at all, do you?" The blonde stepped closer, towering over her. "You were so superior and scornful, simply because I had admitted I wanted a wealthy husband."

"No, I never—"

"Don't bother to deny it. We both know it's true. At least with all my faults, I'm honest. I could admit to the world what I wanted. Can you say the same?"

"Lisa—"

"Because I was truthful, you decided I was shallow and stupid. Jamie, did you ever hear me say I didn't want love? Did I ever say money alone was enough?"

"No."

"You're right, I didn't. Sure, I wanted a wealthy man, but I want him to love *me*. I want it to be my name on his lips when he kisses me, not another. I don't want the man I love to constantly carry the locket that belongs to another woman."

"You mean—"

"You're never far from his thoughts."

"But this trip! He took you."

"Strictly a business trip," Lisa drawled. "Chuck Jordan was scheduled to go and I'm his secretary now. I've traveled with him for weeks. Out of the blue Mike bumped him and took the trip. He used to do all the traveling before."

"Before he met me?"

"Yes."

"Why are you telling me all this?" Jamie looked at Lisa suspiciously. "You have an open field. You're an attractive woman, you could make him fall in love with you."

"Idiot! Don't you think that if I had a chance, I'd try? I've known from the first that it was hopeless."

"How could you?"

"Jamie, who do you think called the reporters that first day?"

"It was you?"

Lisa nodded. "I'll admit to not very commendable motives. I'd seen you and Mike as he carried you into the building. There was something about his look ... Well, I wanted to stop it. I knew from past history that if ever a relationship became public, he dropped the woman. So I tried to cut you out by calling the reporters."

"Mike didn't find out?"

"He found out. He came to me and explained how it was with him. He was kinder than I deserved. Instead of firing me, he offered me a transfer, with a chance to travel and meet the kind of man I wanted."

"And now you have a chance with Mike."

"No." Lisa laughed sarcastically. "I tried it once. I even thought I'd succeeded, but it was your name he called when he kissed me. No, Jamie, I can't fight that."

"Why are you telling me all this?" Jamie asked for a second time.

Lisa ignored her question. "We're due to leave again early in the morning. Mike will be home alone tonight. You have one more chance. If you have any sense at all, you'll take it."

As the words sank into Jamie's befuddled brain she realized incredulously the gift Lisa was offering. Surging to her feet, she threw her arms about the taller woman. "Thank you, Lisa. You may have given me back my life."

"Then I'm glad." Lisa patted her awkwardly on the back.

"You've done so much for me already, could I ask one more favor of you?"

"I'll do anything I can."

"Would you give him this note?" Jamie sat at her desk and scribbled a brief message.

> *Mike,*
> *I need you.*
> *Jamie*

Wanting to laugh, but afraid, Jamie sat hugging herself, loving Meg and Lisa and the world in general. Soon Lisa would be delivering her note. Would he come? He had promised that if ever she needed him, he would be there.

There was one more thing she had to do before she prepared herself for tonight. Suzy Sanderson had been kind in the last weeks. The only article she had published about their stumbling relationship had simply suggested it was a wise cooling-off period, a time for being certain. Jamie dialed the number with a steady hand, not sure at all she knew what she was doing.

A quiet step sounded on the patio tiles. Only one. She knew he was there, waiting. Slowly she turned, stifling a startled gasp at the haggard features visible in the fading light. The flashing green eyes were cold and murky, the light gone from them, and there was no laughter.

"Mike." His name trembled on her lips like a tear.

He acknowledged with a curt nod. "Jamie."

Her eyes, hungry for the sight of him, roved his carefully groomed hair. No unruly locks needed smoothing back tonight. Her heart lurched in compassion at the lines of fatigue marking his taut mouth. As always it was a shock to realize how massive he was. Despite an obvious weight loss, he was still a giant of a man. Even now, standing utterly still, poised and calm, he was overwhelmingly male. A well-tailored shirt was tucked neatly into equally well-tailored trousers. Not a hair out of place, not a crease or a wrinkle, and not the slightest flicker softened his cool, distant facade. He was the ultimate in untouchable control, and she shivered beneath his implacable gaze.

"You look tired." She blurted the words before she could stop them.

"You said you needed me." He spoke quietly, never looking away from her face.

"I do." In spite of her firm resolve to be strong, her voice quavered and dipped to little more than a whisper.

"Are you ill?"

"No." Her hair swung gently across her shoulders as she shook her head in denial. "I'm well."

Only then did his eyes leave hers. Slowly, with infinite care, they searched her face, then dropped to linger at her breasts. Jamie knew he saw the effects of his scrutiny as her nipples quickened beneath the piercing assessment. A flush spread over her neck and cheeks but she refused to flinch or give ground. Falsely, defiantly calm, she stood proudly, letting him see her desire. Carefully, slower still, the penetrating gaze moved over the silken fabric fitted so lovingly over her body. The dress was blatantly provocative; she had meant it to be. It was an invitation; she had meant it to be. She steeled herself as he insolently continued his inspection. From hair to face, from breast to thigh, and back again, lingering at her abdomen, his gaze traveled over her, settling again on her face. Their eyes met and held. His shaded with sadness, hers imploring.

"Are you pregnant?"

Was there the slightest tremor in his voice? Was there, for an instant, a flash of fire in his eyes? Was there the lilt of hidden hope? Jamie bit her lip and swallowed, her parched throat convulsing wildly.

"Not yet."

With bone-deep weariness the gold-tipped lashes dropped, hiding from sight the expression in his eyes. For the first time Mike seemed vulnerable. It was now or never. Jamie knew this was her last chance.

"But if you could forget what a fool I've been, we could remedy that," she answered in a soft murmur of sound.

"Oh, God, honey, don't!" An agitated hand raked through the brown hair, marring its perfection. A single lock fell over his forehead and Jamie smiled. Honey! He had called her honey. This was no longer the stranger with the closed, haunted face, but Mike. Her Mike.

"A little girl with dark hair and green eyes," she

suggested softly, and stepped closer. "Or a rowdy brown-haired boy, almost bigger than his mother."

Mike was ashen now, his eyes still closed. Gathering her courage, Jamie touched him. Her clammy fingers stroked away the deep creases between his brows and smoothed back the beloved curl.

Aware of his unwilling response, she smiled to herself. "I happen to know from experience that this beautiful house has a lovely king-size bed in the master bedroom."

"Stop it, Jamie!" The lashes lifted and his eyes bored into hers. His hand shot out to capture her wrist, as he shrank from her touch. "Do you think I'm made of stone?"

"I certainly hope not." Her silvery laugh floated through the garden as she ignored the pain in her wrist.

"What are you trying to do to me?" His harsh voice rained words on her like hammer blows.

"Frankly I rather thought that was obvious, and I would've preferred the bedroom, but . . ." Refusing to be daunted by his bitterness, she lifted her free hand to the ties at her neck. Slowly she pulled the silken cord.

"Do you know what you're doing?" His hungry eyes were riveted on the loop slipping free.

"That seems to be one of your favorite questions tonight," she answered, half smiling. "And yes, I do know what I'm doing. I'm asking you to make love to me."

"There's more to it than that," he said in a voice rough with feeling.

"Much more," Jamie agreed, stopping her hand. The merest fraction of the knot remained intact. Only its sheer defiance of gravity held the dress over her breasts. "I've faced some real truths about myself these past weeks. For the first time I've realized that at the most crucial and important times of my life, I have always stood alone, and that I wanted it that way. Even in the midst of my family and before audiences, there was only myself and my own ambition."

She hesitated, then continued with determination. "I can see now that even though I thought I wanted him, I couldn't give enough of myself to David. I couldn't let anyone into that private part of my heart and soul, until you. You demanded my all, and I was afraid. Mike, the things I said to you were desperate, pitiful excuses to avoid the truth."

"And now?"

She looked at him fully, reserving nothing. "I'm asking you to hold me. I want to laugh with you. I want you to protect me and let me, in my own way, protect you. I want your strength and gentleness for my own. I want to fight with you. I want to be friend and lover. I want to be there when you reach out in the night and wake with you by my side each morning. If you are man, I want to be woman—and I want you to teach me not to be afraid."

Jamie paused, breathless from her impassioned plea. She waited for a response, some sign that he had heard the cry from her heart, and understood. There was only the chirping of a cricket, the soft lapping of the water in the pool, and the painful beat of her heart to break the stillness. She waited.

"That's a tall order." His quiet words broke the silence.

"You're a tall man."

"I'm not sure we could make it work."

"Yes, we can, but only if you give me what I want most in the world. Your love."

His reply was low and quiet. "You've had that for a long time."

"I know that . . . now."

"I'll probably forget what a strong woman you are for such a little thing." A tiny glint kindled in his eyes and in the shadows they seemed to clear and glow brilliantly green.

"I'll remind you."

"I'll forget and hover over you with my gallant act."

"I expect it, feathered hat and all."

"I'll be irritable."

"And I'll be stubborn."

"We'll fight."

"Think of the delicious fun of making up."

"One of us should call Suzy."

"I already did."

"Pretty sure of yourself, weren't you?"

"No, desperate."

"Our daughters will probably be six foot five and our sons five foot nothing."

"They wouldn't dare!" The laughter was back. It sparkled in his eyes. With joy in her heart she watched it flare into full blaze and grow. The strain in his face eased and the grim mouth was now shaped into the familiar lines of his smile. Jamie knew her own face was lit with laughter as it flowed effervescently through her.

"Jamie?" The lips were no longer smiling; his expression was deadly earnest.

"What is it?" Her spirits, which had so recently soared, plummeted.

"I have one very important question I must ask."

"What—what question?" She stammered, searching her mind for some reason for this sudden change in him.

"Do you—" He paused, hesitated, looked significantly at her hand still holding the cord of silk at her nape. "Do you need any help with that tie?"

"Do I need any help?" She frowned, her muddled mind not registering the return of the teasing note in his words. "Help with the tie?" Then she caught the wicked mischief in his grin. "Oooh, you! You frightened me out of my wits. You . . . you . . ."

"Crazy?" Mike supplied, the grin widening.

"Yes, crazy."

"Sweet?" he dared.

"Sweet." She nodded.

"Wonderful?" He grew bolder.

"Ah, yes, wonderful."

"Irresistible?" This time hopefully.

"Totally," she agreed.

"And you love me," he added firmly.

"Yes, I do. I love you very much." A sweet, pale radiance suffused her. Her very soul seemed to glow with a deep abiding happiness.

Slowly, gently, Mike took the tie from her hand. With the barest tug, the knot released, yielding at last to the laws of gravity. In a slither of silken color, the dress fell in a pool about her feet. Jamie stood in the moonlight, clad only in the delicate chain that held the sapphire ring nestled between her breasts.

"My beautiful Jamie." He touched her then, gathering her to him as he buried his face in her hair. Effortlessly he swung her high into his arms. Pausing at every step to kiss her hungrily, he made his way through the house, his destination the master suite.

Hours later, lying in a tangle of arms and legs, Jamie's head rested against his shoulder, her hair a dark swath across his chest.

"Why did you cut it?" He held a fragrant curl against his lips.

"An impulse. Do you mind?"

"No."

"But I thought you liked it long."

"I did. It was lovely, but I hated the burden it was to you. Don't forget, I saw how much trouble it could be. I saw how at times it seemed to weigh you down."

"And you really don't mind?"

"Only if you cut it because of what happened."

"I didn't do it out of spite, Mike. It wasn't because of what happened at the pool."

"I was afraid it had become an unpleasant reminder."

"Unpleasant reminder! Of the most beautiful night of my life?"

"Most beautiful night? Explain," he commanded.

"Until I started acting cowardly and pigheaded, it was, and until tonight."

"Tonight?" he prompted, a slow satisfied smile spreading across his face.

"Even you have to admit tonight has been pretty spectacular."

"Only spectacular? You wound me."

"Perhaps if you keep trying, you can do better. Let's call it your birthday celebration."

"It's not my birthday."

"When did that ever stop you?" She smiled innocently. Her palm traced a seductive path across his chest as she admired the sapphire ring Mike had placed on her finger. "But then maybe you're too tired."

"Witch! I'll show you who's tired. I'll give you spectacular and more." In one swoop Jamie found herself flat on her back. Mike leaned near, laughing down at her. With loving fingers she stroked the shape of his lips. He brushed a kiss on the finger the ring encircled.

"Did you know this ring is the exact color of your eyes." His hand slipped to her breasts, teasing a dusky nipple into tingling desire.

"N—no."

"I knew I had to have you the day I found it."

"You knew even then?"

"Especially then."

"It's a lovely ring."

"We'll get it sized tomorrow."

"Good. It looks much better on my hand than it did hidden away on a chain," Jamie declared.

"I'm not so sure about that. As I recall, it rested right about here." He pressed a tender kiss to the spot where the ring had lain between her breasts. "I can't think of a better place to be."

"Mmm." Jamie writhed beneath his searching lips. The rasp of his tongue against a sensitive nipple drew an even deeper sigh from her. Her own lips sought and found his vulnerable places.

"Ah, my lovely Jamie, woman is thy name," Mike breathed into her hair.

"That's beautiful." She relaxed against him, enjoying his touch. "Who said it?"

"I think I just did."

"Ah-ha! Aren't you the smart one? You . . . you . . ." She snuggled closer against him as she searched for the proper insult.

"Jamie, my love." Mike tilted her chin, his eyes twinkling down at her, his lips twitching with a repressed smile. "You talk too much."

Her laughter filled the darkened room. "You're absolutely right, I do. What're we going to do about it?"

"For starters how about this?" Mike answered as he applied himself to the task. "And this?"

"And this?"

"Or this?"

"Mike."

"Now, Jamie. Now your eyes are violet."

About the Author

BJ JAMES is an author whose books from Loveswept and Silhouette consistently place in the top ranks of best-seller lists at the chain bookstores. She has twice been honored by the Georgia Romance Writers with their prestigious Maggie Award for Best Short Contemporary Romance, and she has also received the *Romantic Times* Critic's Choice Award. BJ lives in North Carolina with her high school sweetheart husband.